Further
From
Home

FURTHER FROM HOME

A Collection of *Philosophical* Short Stories

Thomas Dylan Daniel, M. A.

Thank you for reading. If you enjoy this book, please leave a review or connect with the author.

Interior Design by Nicole R. Locker

FOREWORD

It is important to think, as we live our lives. As Socrates said, the unexamined life is not worth living. This concept reverberates through the whole of human thought, if we pay attention to it. Zen Buddhism maintains the importance of awareness to life even as Taoism and contemporary self-help gurus do. To do, and be aware as we do, is the key to not only success but also to happiness in doing. How do we become aware? How do we stay that way?

Zen monks would maintain that there is no set recipe. It is not a thing which can be explained, and thus we are to kill the Buddha if we meet him on the road. No one will solve the mystery for us. And no one can tell us how to do it. Rather, we must venture into puzzlement until we become aware of the solution for ourselves. Each person's path is different.

This collection of short stories is the product of many years' writing, reading, and conversation. Its purpose is to puzzle the reader in a beneficial, amusing, and fun way. It is targeted at young Americans because I have written it for and to my younger self. I hope a broader audience finds it palatable, but I am unwilling to modify its content or water it down to sell more copies.

It is the goal of this little book to pry open the reader's mind by beginning in the most seemingly mundane of conceptual realms and moving forward, slowly, imperceptibly, and gradually into unfamiliar territory.

Beginning with a short story about sleepwalking and guns, we move into more explicitly philosophical territory with a few stories about philosophers and chess, academia and gambling. Then, we see the difficulty in changing a person's political views and look at meaning in life through a variety of lenses before slipping into solipsism and melancholy. The final story is meant to snap the reader out of the spell by directing focus back to what matters: self-reference, recursion, self-awareness. Humanity's place in the world is special because we are a mechanism by which world perceives itself.

Philosophy is a strange, difficult, and arcane subject at times, but it is possible to grow by understanding and through introspection. This is a strange, inexplicable book. As I read through it, I feel as though someone else has written it and not me. I chose not to publish it under a pseudonym, even though some of the content makes me uncomfortable.

In the end, these are stories which make me smile, and make me laugh, and which make me more aware of what it means to be myself. Perhaps they will cause a similar reaction in you.

Table of Contents

x

NEVER WAKE A SLEEPWALKER

Hannah and Dawn were sisters. They'd purchased a timeshare in Ruidoso years before, as Dawn had moved to LA with her husband Jonathan and Hannah had opted to remain in Dallas. Dawn's wealth had grown significantly as her agency had expanded, but Hannah was nearly broke. The timeshare was like a financial cancer – she was unable to part with it, or to ask her sister for help, even as the expense of the place caused her to be late on other bills.

Hannah was a recent divorcee, and her children Tony and Sarah were 10 and 9 years old respectively. Dawn had three children, but they were older and had appointments and camps to attend during the summer, so she came alone.

Dawn was an avid proponent of firearms. She travelled with a gun in her glove compartment, one under her seat, and at least three other stashed in her pockets, purse, and luggage.

Hannah wasn't sure what to make of this new development. Perhaps Dawn had undergone some trauma, she reflected, as her sister finished pouring them both another glass of wine. The kids, tired from the drive, had already gone to sleep an hour or so before, and Hannah was not far behind them.

The next morning, the sun shone down through the trees before everyone was awake. Tony was the last out of bed. In the course of his love affair with video games, he had already developed the habit of sleeping until at least 10:00 whenever this was possible. Sarah joined her mother and her aunt Dawn in the kitchen as soon as the sounds of the older women making breakfast woke her.

"Wait, so you think Tony got into the wine?" she asked, groggily.

"Well, we'll see when he wakes up. It was on top of the refrigerator," Hannah pointed to the jug of Carlo Rossi sangria that sat, mostly empty, on its side, near the sink.

"It wasn't me," Dawn joked, happily. She opened the oven and pulled out a tray of biscuits.

Sarah sat at the table, staring at the wine from across the room. She poured herself a bowl of Cheerios and dumped some milk into it.

"Yeah, I didn't touch that either. I was too tired." Hannah yawned, cradling a cup of coffee between her hands.

Tony, Hannah knew, was almost always a bit of a grouch when he woke up in the mornings. She watched him, as he entered the room, almost in a daze. He took a glass from the cupboard and poured himself some water from the tap, sipping it as he sat down across the table from her. Dawn handed him a plate with a biscuit on it, and he took a knife to it. Hannah supplied her son with jelly and watched as he spread a bit of it on each half of his biscuit. He seemed groggy, but not hung over. As the four of them went through the day, hiking, telling stories, and eating meals together, Hannah wondered why she was so preoccupied with the disappearance of their wine supply. Dawn had always been prone to sleepwalking,

2

a trait which Sarah seemed to have inherited, but at least Tony hadn't gotten drunk. Of that, she was sure.

The second night was off to a start that resembled the first. The cabin was quiet, except for Hannah and Dawn's low conversation on the patio and the chirping of crickets. Hannah's divorce was recently final, but she artfully steered the conversation back to the wine. It struck Dawn that perhaps the two of them were avoiding the divorce deliberately.

"I'm going to put it in the cupboard tonight," Dawn was saying. They'd purchased a second gallon of the stuff during the day, and had barely just finished the first. The trip was supposed to last another two nights, and Dawn didn't want to find herself without alcohol.

"That sounds good. Make sure you put it high up, keep the kids out." Hannah bit off a yawn. "It's time for me to go to bed."

"Good night," Dawn replied, as her sister got up and left her alone on the porch. She had a plan. Ever the sleepwalker herself, Dawn knew that there was a chance one of the kids had developed the behavior as a result of the stress of the divorce.

It seemed like only a few minutes had passed, but the crickets had gone silent. Inside the cabin, something was moving around, with the lights still off. Suddenly, there was a loud *thud*. Dawn jerked open the patio door, flipped on the lights. Nobody was there. Hannah came creeping out of her bedroom.

"Have you seen Tony?"

"No, Dawn. What was that noise?" Hannah rubbed her eyes.

3

Sarah came out of the kids' room, and Hannah repeated the question.

"No, mom." Sarah didn't seem very groggy. The sudden awakening had jolted her into a state of alertness. She walked to the front door, tried the knob. It was still locked. She strode across the living room, into Dawn's room. The older women followed. When they reached Dawn's room, Hannah flipped on the light switch.

Sarah stood behind her brother, with her hands on his shoulders. Aunt Dawn's purse was on the floor next to his feet, and a 9MM pistol was still in his hands. As they watched, Sarah gently slid the gun out her brother's hand and dropped it on the floor. The sound woke Tony, whose first instinct was to lash out.

A few minutes later, they all sat together in the kids' room. There was a bag of frozen fruit for Sarah's eye.

"I'm glad you took the gun before he woke up," Dawn was saying, as she studied the firearm. "He had taken off the safety. Someone could have been killed."

THE PHILOSOPHER'S RIDDLE

I first met the philosopher when I was young; maybe fourteen years old or thereabouts. That fine August day, I was walking home from school with a friend. We went into an alley, along the way, and Darren took an empty coke can and a baggy of marijuana out of his backpack. I turned away, aghast at the idea of changing my mind with chemicals, and ran. I ran down the street, turned the corner, and went into a coffee shop; and that is where I met the old man.

"You look as if you've seen a ghost," he confronted me.

I looked down at my shirt, covered in sweat. I wanted to cry, but instead I sat down.

"I haven't," I said.

"Well, are you in school? Who are you running from? Do you need help?" he asked, the edge of a grin on his face.

"No," I replied. "I'm alright. I just need a minute."

He went to the counter to get me a glass of water. When he returned, he took a seat across the table from me. I looked at him, for the first time, after my first drink of cold water. He wore a blazer and a long beard, but he was balding. I could tell because his long hair hung out the back of his hat but not from the front or sides. He was fat, but not overly so, and his dark green eyes awaited the end of my appraisal with great patience.

"I'm Murray," I said, extending a hand.

"I'm John," he replied, clutching my palm in his own.

"Well, John, I feel better now. Thank you for the water."

"Why, certainly, Murray. It was no trouble," the man smiled.

"Who are you?" I asked, in the timeless arrogance of youth.

"My name is John. I'm a philosopher," the man said.

"What's a philosopher?" I asked.

"A philosopher. Hmm. Philosophy entails an open-minded view of the world, with an eye for detail and a general opposition to biases or prejudice," he said.

A brief moment passed, and he nodded again.

"Yes, that's about what it means, these days."

"So you don't know what you are, but you try not to jump to conclusions about things?"

I honestly had no difficulty wrapping my head around this. After my shake-up, this seemed almost comforting.

The man nodded.

"Well, thanks for the water," I said. I hadn't intended to take longer than usual to get home, and stood to leave.

"Yes, Murray. It was no trouble. Nice meeting you," he said with a bit more of that grin sneaking out.

As I walked out of the coffee shop, it occurred to me that the man was not like other adults. He hadn't pried, he hadn't scolded me. I left the coffee shop that afternoon with a healthy resolve to avoid drugs and the friends who used them, but I felt a good deal less anxious. And I barely thought another thought about the philosopher. He simply seemed to fit.

As the years went on, I studied hard in school. I went to church, and I did not waver in my desire to remain sober. The second time I saw him, I was seventeen. He remembered me, though I had forgotten him entirely.

I was in the bookstore in the mall, looking through the self-help section for a bit of advice about women. He stood in the next section over, perusing the philosophy books there. I chose a volume and began to read the back jacket, but he addressed me in a booming voice.

"Excuse me, young man!" he exclaimed, startling me.

My cheeks instantly turned red. Who was this? How had I been caught?

"I believe we've met somewhere," he stated; a plain truth.

I almost ran. Instead, I hastily tucked the book I had chosen back into position on the shelf.

"Ehrm," I said. "I don't believe we have." I avoided his stare.

He was not to be dissuaded.

"Yes, you're the lad from the coffee shop that day. The one who was running from something." He paused for a moment, watching me squirm as I attempted to recollect him without looking him in the eye. "I wonder, did you make good your escape?"

I could feel his eyes boring into the top of my head like lasers as I examined his shoes. They were leather, but old. He clearly wore them on a daily basis, but they had originated as dress shoes. Light brown, well worn, and yet very nice – the tops still had a shine to them, even though the toes and insteps were scuffed to bits. I looked up, curious about the owner of the shoes, into a strangely familiar face.

I looked away, staring at the books on the shelves as though the answer to my question could be found there.

My embarrassment was compounded by my inability to remember where I had seen this man, and as I searched my soul for a reply to his question, I found myself mute. I thought, strangely, of the man who had used to bring lemon drops to church when I was seven or eight. He had been very old, and very slow, but had cared enough about the kids to bring us candy. He was almost certainly dead, by now, I noted. My grandfather had been his friend. Then, in the blink of an eye, it dawned upon me!

"Why, you're the philosopher!" I remarked, beaming at my success. I met his eye, for the first time in years. "I remember now!"

"You see? It's a small world, after all." He shrugged, turning away. He was apparently ready to let the conversation go and get back to his search.

"What kind of books are you looking for? And, what's a philosopher?" I almost kept asking questions, but it occurred to me that this would have been rude, so I silenced myself with an act of will.

He turned back to me, smiling.

"Why, a philosopher is someone who pays very careful attention to words. Philosophy itself comes from the Greek: *philo* means 'love of' and *sophia* means 'wisdom.' I'm looking for information about David Hume, but there isn't much here." He gestured to the shelves disapprovingly. "They don't have anything good at the library either. I'm afraid I may have to use the internet."

He exhaled, loudly. With a sad gesture toward the ceiling, he turned to face me.

"What about you? What sort of wisdom do you hope to find here?"

"Well, I'm..." I trailed off. I needed to quickly think of a cover story.

Adeptly, the philosopher reached for the shelf and pulled out the book I'd been about to have a look at.

"The Art of Kissing," he said with an air of wonder. "You're looking for help with romance, aren't you?" He grinned at me.

I shrugged. "Well, you see, there's this girl I like and I'm supposed to see her this weekend, but I don't know much about any of that, and so..." I allowed myself to trail off. The grin was growing wider.

"Let me help you. You're not quite sure how to think of a plan for a situation you've never encountered before, and so you're looking for a map, a map built of words, to help you chart your course!"

Puzzled, I shrugged a bit.

"I was just hoping to learn about kissing so that I wouldn't be bad at it, if it came to that," I replied.

"Haha!" said the philosopher. "You know, you're on an interesting path." He handed me the book. "Words are very powerful, very powerful indeed. With them, we can teach each other the how and the why of almost anything. It's important to remember, though, that words have their limit. They can only teach us theory, never practice."

He paused for a long moment, then handed me the book.

"With words, we can control a great deal of the world," he said.

"Can we? Is that real?" I asked, intrigued.

"Why, of course! Why do you think so much of magic involves spoken words?" Here, he paused. He wanted a response.

"Well, I'm not sure about magic, but I know the Bible instructs us against it."

"Certainly. But how does it go about that?"

"Well," I thought for a moment. "With words?"

"Ha! Yes! Absolutely," said the philosopher.

"I suppose that isn't uncommon, but you seem to mean something beyond it," I said. It was a lame attempt to reach my point, but he followed.

"You're most certainly correct! Words are far more powerful than they seem at first glance. Do you have a cellphone?"

I reached into my pocket, pulling out my touchscreen smartphone. I pushed the button to turn its display on and showed it to him.

"What makes it work?" the philosopher asked.

"Why, it has a microprocessor, an internet connection, an operating system…"

He was motioning for me to continue with his hand. When I stopped, he decided to help me out.

"Well, sure, it has all of those things. It's really quite remarkable! What does it do?"

"It connects to the internet and runs applications…?"

10

I shrugged to indicate that I wasn't sure what he was getting at.

"Why, of course it does! Very good! But what makes all of that possible in the first place?"

"Electricity?"

"No, boy! Words! Words make it possible. The conceptual framework, reduced to the abstract, is what makes it all possible in the first place." He chuckled a bit.

"I see," I said, though I didn't. This man must be insane. How could something as simple as a word be the backbone of a smartphone? Plus, wasn't binary composed of ones and zeroes? There was a riddle, here, but I didn't know where to begin.

I excused myself from his company and left the store, purchasing my kissing book. The book was educational. That weekend, I was pleased by my opportunity to use its advice – and disappointed that it had been virtually no help at all. Gradually, I stopped wondering what the strange old man meant about the power of words. I'd read them, and it hadn't prepared me adequately, so I decided that he must be wrong.

The third time I saw the philosopher, I had enrolled for my second semester of classes at the university. He was to teach my Introduction to Philosophy course. This time, he appeared to have forgotten me. My ear got that peculiar ringing sensation, the one my mother used to associate with people talking about me, as I walked to class on the first day. I waved to a few friends, hurrying along through the damp January morning. My breath made fog in the air. Finally, I reached the philosophy building. I was five minutes early when I pushed open the door to the classroom and stepped in. There he was, joking around with some of the other students.

That was the hardest class I took, during all my years of college. We read Hobbes' account of ratiocination. We read Mill about liberty. We read Aquinas about five ways that God's existence could be proven and Descartes about mind/body relations. It was my first 'B' and I found myself painfully embarrassed to have earned it. I went to the philosopher's office, intending to ask him about the grade, having mainly avoided him during the semester.

"Murray, hello," he said warmly, turning his gaze up from the book he was reading.

I wasn't sure whether he'd looked up first, or whether he'd spoken my name first. In either case, the self-assured air he projected seemed to indicate a familiarity with the idea of my coming to his office for a visit.

"Hi, John," I replied. I should have addressed him as Dr. Gilbertson, but for some reason his first name came to mind more easily.

He motioned for me to have a seat.

"How are you?" he asked. I was a little surprised – among my classmates, he had a reputation for avoiding small-talk.

"I've been well. I'm troubled, though. By my grade." I was downtrodden, by it, in fact.

I thought of my final essay, marked with a big red C, in my bag. I didn't reach for it, because I knew I had failed to articulate my point clearly. Flashing through my mind, my account of the Five Ways and its marriage to Hobbes rewound itself to the day the essay was assigned, over three weeks ago. My time, sunk into that project, appeared wasted to me in that moment, as the anger swelled up in my chest. *How dare this man accuse me of being wrong! I spent so much time!*

My thoughts parted, and I realized the professor was speaking to me.

"Murray, you're a bright student. The trouble is all in your approach to the words." He managed to appear grave, even as he uttered such a silly sentence. "I can't tell you much more plainly than that. You're guilty of making leaps, and I simply cannot award you top marks for it. It means you're missing the point of the class." His eyes softened a bit. It was clear that he was trying to explain.

It was no use, though. I was baffled. The words? I wracked my brain, trying to comprehend what he'd said. I was used to more direction from my professors.

"But, sir, I don't understand. Just as I didn't at the bookstore."

"Yes, I was afraid of that. You know, not everyone does. And that's okay. For my part, I was hoping we'd have this visit earlier in the semester, but I understand – you're not the type to make a 'B' and you didn't think it would come to this. Really, though, you just didn't excel as much as some of the other students. If you're hoping I'll change your grade, I'm afraid I have to tell you I won't." He folded his hands onto one another atop his desk, then leaned back in his chair.

"It isn't the grade, really," I began. "It's the befuddlement. What is all of this supposed to mean? We've looked at many different thinkers, we've

13

analyzed their essays and the concepts they left behind. You say you're teaching me analytic philosophy, but I'm not even sure what that means – and I've completed your class!" I could feel my pulse speeding as I spoke, and try as I might to contain myself, it just kept accelerating. "If you're not going to tell me what to do, or how to do it, or even what the class is about – then what's the point of my attendance? How am I supposed to excel if I don't know what I'm doing here?" Nearly shouting, I found myself standing up.

I was leaning over the desk, irately venting my emotions onto the stoic professor.

He never even blinked.

I calmed myself, before continuing: "I put everything into my final paper. You accuse me of making leaps but I don't understand why; I shore them up with arguments and I demonstrate their veracity with logic."

"Murray; I've told you this before. I've lectured about it, and I've brought it up to you in conversation. Words are phenomenally powerful, and they are so in a way unlike anything else. Philosophers must respect them, but you misuse them. You overstate your points. If your paper held true under analysis, it would be the shortest and most significant essay in history – a reputation it unfortunately does not merit. Do you understand what I mean by that?" His eyes bored into mine, intensely.

I turned, pacing back toward the door of the small office. I turned again, walking toward the desk. When I reached it, I pivoted and continued my stroll. The second time I approached the desk, I began to quote aloud.

"A word is more than a mere symbol. Although its relevance to its subject is arbitrary, its influence upon said subject is not. Thus, as a word progresses through its life-cycle, it can find itself in a variety of situations – some appropriate, and others not so much." I had memorized the opening lecture he gave. It had been my only hope of survival in the class – but I knew I still hadn't managed to crack the riddle the philosopher had posed, in words, at the bookstore.

"Very good, Murray," he congratulated me.

I turned to stare at him, more frustrated with myself than with him.

"But do you understand what I meant by that?" He inserted a meaningful pause, here, then continued. "Ninety-five percent of those students either never listened to that lecture or forgot it. You've clearly been contextualizing it, reading it into the bizarre history you and I share. But you wouldn't be here if you'd worked it out." He pushed his chair back further, kicked his feet up onto the desk. "What is it about the words?"

I sat back down, forced to confront the reality of repeating the same trite trope.

"That they're invented for specific purposes, but they fulfill those roles and then take on a life of their own, in turn changing the world? That they're thus anything but arbitrary."

He continued staring at me, but remained mute.

I shrugged. He'd already told me he wouldn't change the grade. What could I lose?

"Sir, I have questioned my faith, this semester! I've questioned my existence. I've questioned – honestly, truthfully, and maddeningly, my own free will! I don't know what more I can do for you," I finished my plea with a plaintive sigh, raising my hands with the palms up.

"You just need to put it all together. Each of the questions you listed is rooted in a word; but you're hanging onto the concepts the words represent."

He cleared his throat, making a little gesture with his hand.

I sat up a little straighter, attempting to glean something I could apply to myself from his critique.

"You're allowing yourself to be pulled by the love of a concept into admitting false properties of its symbol," he added with a shrug. "When you let that go, you'll understand what you were missing here. It's a conflation."

I couldn't understand. I was upset, and irritated, and I thought we'd discussed this before.

His gaze softened as he read the depressed look on my face. "A 'B' is a fine grade in a philosophy class and I appreciate your efforts this semester." Apparently deciding to let me off the hook, he dismissed me with a little wave of his hand. "Please, keep in touch!"

I could feel myself turning red. I snatched my bag, stormed to the door of the little office, jerked it open, and slammed it behind me. My anger didn't last forever, though. The next August, I returned to campus. I went to see my old nemesis again, thinking perhaps I had solved the riddle, but the philosopher was gone. Disappeared. Retired. He'd simply quit his job and moved away, leaving me with an empty office to address my embarrassment to. I had a theory about what I had been missing, but I would have the rest of my life to come up with the right answers. It was frustrating, but my need for instant gratification, for confirmation, would have to go unmet.

DUE TO THE STORM

Mark sat at the bench in the park where Bobby Fischer had once sat. He was surrounded by blue skies, recently cut May grass, tall trees and the intermittent sounds of birds and cars and people. Everyone was enjoying this, the finest of New York City spring afternoons. Directly in front of the bench sat a chess board on a table where a mature game unfolded.

Staring into the depths of this game, Mark's grandfather sat across from him. At seventy-three years old, Albert was not what he had been physically, although his acumen remained intact and sharper than ever. His grandson was taking philosophy classes at the university and he relished the opportunity to challenge the young man's developing skills.

He moved a pawn. Looking up, he prepared to voice his thoughts on a conversation that had been unfolding even longer than the game they sat immersed in.

"Nietzsche gave power to Hitler. That's what you youngsters just don't seem to understand; there is something very wrong about attacking society in the way he did. The wounds you open provide malice with a means of ingress."

Mark listened to the words without looking at his grandfather. He was tanned and lean, a youth of some nineteen years, enraptured by the metaphysics of

Heidegger and the poetic anti-Christian rants of Nietzsche. He straightened up in his seat without moving a piece and looked directly into the blue eyes and weathered face of his grandfather. The man was a chess master who had studied philosophy in his own youth, but to Mark he seemed somehow scarred by the extensive dealings he had had with the business world as he worked to support his family.

"Those things, the devices Hitler used, they are all around us! You can get them from the Bible, for God's sake!" he exclaimed.

Albert's gaze narrowed in response, but he held his tongue.

Mark noted the old man's indignation. He took a breath and continued: "Nietzsche was the greatest philosopher ever to live; his philosophy expressed what he saw in the world! Not the way it should be." He moved a bishop to attack.

"Ah," said Albert. It was unclear to Mark whether the response addressed the move or the statement. He looked up from the board. "Isn't society what keeps men like Hitler from taking charge? We suffer the fools because they are handicapped; but we must vet the leaders carefully. This should apply to philosophers as well, because they have such tremendous influence over those in power." Triumphant, he took the young man's bishop with his own.

Mark's thoughts raced, but he paused for a long moment to formulate a careful reply. His respect for his grandfather exceeded any difference that could exist between them. Before he could begin to speak, however, a loud thunderclap interrupted him. Briefly forgetting the game and the conversation, the two men looked skyward in unison.

"Pack up the men and board, Mark."

Mark did as he was instructed as his grandfather stood upright, leaning heavily upon his cane. When all of the pieces were in their bag, the board was rolled up, and the set was stowed inside Mark's backpack, the two men walked back toward the entrance of the park.

"There's the spot," Albert said as they laconically approached a diner. Just then the rain started, small drops at first. The air smelled sweetly, but almost immediately a howling wind followed this initial barrage. Larger and larger drops began to fall until it was difficult to see the diner across the street. Mark put his arm around his grandfather for support and helped him cross the street to where the coffee and sweet rolls awaited.

The two men sat down in a booth that was sufficiently far away from the door, then took out the chess board and pieces. Mark put in the order, the waitress standing at the end of the booth. Albert began to set up the pieces exactly as they had been before the storm forced them into the bag. The waitress bustled away and Mark turned to watch his grandfather deciding where the remaining few pieces went with a smile upon his face.

"Grandfather," he said. "You took my bishop with yours. It does not belong upon the board anymore."

The grandfather winked and smiled at Mark. "You're still young enough to be honest, I see." He removed the white bishop, putting his black one where it had been, smiling the whole time. Mark had never beaten him. When the board was set just right, he decided to restart the conversation.

"Mark," he said, taking a serious tone, "you must be careful when deciding upon your opinions and affiliations."

He turned aside to accept a cup of coffee from the pretty waitress, who had reappeared, smiling at the two men with a knowing twinkle in her eye. Mark quietly smiled back at her as he accepted his coffee. She placed a roll in front of him and walked away, still smiling.

Mark turned to his grandfather and grinned sheepishly.

"Still got it," the old man commented, awaiting Mark's move.

Mark moved a knight. The piece had formerly been tasked with the defense of the king, and his grandfather grunted as he immediately captured the knight with the light-squared bishop from across the board. Neither man said a word. Both sat calculating possibilities, intent upon the changing dynamics of the game.

Mark finally sighed. He reclined, surveying the board, and thinking about his response to the old man's attack upon his idealism.

"Grandfather, there is not a single thing for anyone to believe anymore." He sat up, meeting Albert's gaze. "The world is full of charlatans. Men who respond negatively to them are to be commended. Your point about Hitler highlights the difficulties that even Nietzsche had in grasping the enormity of his task. He used two or perhaps even

21

more ways of interrogating society, but only one of them is truly accessible to everyone."

Mark paused to take a deep breath. He moved a pawn before he continued, working hard to restrain his excitement.

"The reason Hitler was able to subvert Nietzsche's genius was that the masses never truly understood just what he was critiquing. They took the *ubermensch* and turned it into an ideal without understanding that this kind of idealism was precisely what the *ubermensch* was intended to attack! Nietzsche said throw down your idols and the fools misunderstood him, or perhaps misconstrued his meaning, taking his very words as idols themselves!"

Albert listened intently to his grandson's speech. He moved his remaining knight to attack, then sat back to put together a reply.

Mark immediately moved a rook to the end of the board and removed his hand from it. He paused for a moment, then attempted to pick it up again.

Albert swatted his hand away; the move had been made.

"Your mistake, young one, is that you think the world is soft; you overestimate your ability to bend it to your own will," he scolded.

Albert gave Mark a meaningful glance and then reached once again for the chess board. Taking the rook with his bishop, he barked a short laugh. He picked up his coffee and stared at his grandson.

"If you attempt to push the masses in a direction with contempt, they will revolt and you will fail. If you try to push them toward their destruction like Hitler did, they will recoil as surely as if they were pushed toward the ultimate liberal ideal by a clueless youth such as yourself. Who, pray tell, was the first philosopher you studied?"

Conscious of the impact of the mistake he'd made upon the chessboard as well as the cost of his verbosity in the conversation, Mark slouched visibly. The game looked like it might be lost, but perhaps he could salvage his philosophical reputation in the old man's eyes. He'd played too aggressively and was aware of the parallel between his conversation and his chess play. The old man had overextended himself, but the rook move was a costly blunder. Perhaps he could still crack the defense.

"I misspoke, just as I moved without thinking." Mark apologized. He was beginning to sweat. Would the old man think him a fool?

A few moves went by as they sat in silence, mainly trading pawns as Albert consolidated his advantage by opening the center of the board. The game progressed toward its end, and Mark was down by a full rook. Still, the material aside, his dark-square bishop was in position.

Finally, Mark was ready to supply the response the old man awaited.

"Of course, the first philosopher I studied was Plato, and what I learned from him was that I didn't know anything. I learned a system of interrogation I could use to discover what the world was really like. What language was really like. But where Plato used reason to destroy, Aristotle used it to put things together again."

"So, boy, how do you intend to pick up the pieces left by Nietzsche's careless destruction and build a system for people to work and live together?" As he spoke, Albert raised a white eyebrow. He advanced his passed pawn another square.

This analogy was truly the heart of the conversation, and Mark suddenly had an idea for the chess game as well. He whipped his queen across the board, an unexpected move. It was now attacking the king in tandem with the bishop.

Albert smiled as he moved his king out of check. Mark slid his remaining rook down the board. His grandfather was now faced with a dilemma to consider, and Mark was prepared to assume control of the conversation again. He leaned forward as the old man stared at the board.

"Grandfather, why do you assume that Nietzsche's attack left pieces which must be reassembled? If I had shot Hitler, would you advocate me taking him to the hospital?" He popped the last bit of his sweet roll into his mouth and chewed it, watching the old man.

"You must understand, after all, that insecurity is the reason we feel the need to put everyone in their particular place and organize society – but you must also remember that Plato criticized *sophists*, men who were authorities on particular subjects. Couldn't Nietzsche's criticism hold without another authoritative scheme being put into place?" Mark paused, waiting for his grandfather to reply.

"What you're suggesting is anarchy!" cried Albert, turning red. His voice took on a hurt tone as he rejected Mark's idea. He angrily took Mark's queen with a rook as the boy considered the board.

"But, Grandfather, Nietzsche might reply that anarchy has been reality for all these long years! Is it not possible that authority itself is to blame for its abuses?" Mark moved his knight to fork Albert's queen and king, quietly awaiting his elder's response.

The old man moved his king out of check again. His face was red, his movements jerky. He was restraining himself and trying to consider the youth's opinion as valid, but it was beyond his ability.

"To suggest that... you insolent whelp! I fought two wars for your ability to sit here and condemn my efforts! This is... certainly not anarchy! Look what happened with Hurricane Katrina! People are animals when there is nobody to watch them and it takes only seconds to suffer the collapse of everything we've all worked for..." he trailed off.

Mark had moved the bishop, checkmating him for the first time. The king was trapped by a rook on one side and a queen on the other. The only available escape was blocked by the knight Albert had assumed would be taking his queen on the next move.

"Have you forgotten, Grandfather? Nietzsche himself said that a philosopher was a human who constantly experiences, sees, hears, suspects, hopes, and dreams extraordinary things; who is struck by his own thoughts as from outside! How long have they held captive your mind? You study, you read, and yet you subject yourself only to the thoughts of others! The fact is, though we have fallen down in the past as a race, mankind as a whole, led by man the individual, is progressing."

Mark leaned in toward the old man who still stared at the board as if his defeat at the hands of this youth was still not a fact. He was being too loud, but this was his moment of triumph! "When you understand that," he continued more quietly, "you understand that the world is truly dangerous. Neither of us might live to see tomorrow. It is only by our own strength that we continue, collecting our scars in exchange for our survival."

The youth fell silent as the old man's gaze struck him; a gaze that harbored something beyond the contempt it had held just earlier that day. The old man was cantankerous. His repeated successes had left him full of an egoistic bile that he could not help but share, even with his favorite grandson.

Mark saw the glimmer of a smile appear on Albert's face as he excused himself to the restroom. The old man knew, of course, that the Nazis had perverted Nietzsche to use him for their own ends; yet he had always assumed, like everyone else, that Nietzsche himself had precipitated this by attacking the social constructs that maintained the status quo. How could this not have been the end he deliberately set out to serve? Mark shook his head, inwardly cringing as he remembered the lecture he had witnessed the week before.

In fact, Nietzsche praised the Jews for their strength in faith, among many other things – an almost inconceivable irony, given the history of the National Socialist Party that had striven to such lengths to absorb him as one of their own. Anti-Semitism had certainly never been Nietzsche's goal. His association with it indicated a weakness in the reader, not in the author.

Mark began to pack up the chess set. Albert returned to the table, and when Mark looked at him, he was struck by what he saw written plainly across the old man's thoughtful countenance: respect. As the two embarked upon the short journey home, few words were needed to express the new strength of the bond between them.

COQUETRY

C an a camera really steal your soul?" I asked, wondering aloud.

Nearby, a young blonde woman was repeatedly snapping selfies with the forward-facing camera on her iPhone.

Initially, as I sat in the diner, across the table from my dark-haired wife, I had thought the young lady quite beautiful and had even gone so far as to think it strange to see her sitting alone.

Stephanie was nonplussed.

"What's a soul? You're an atheist, Darren. I don't think you have a dog in this fight."

Her face took on an amused, quizzical look that told me she was speaking from sarcasm – and encouraged me to share my thoughts.

"Excuse me, miss," I bellowed.

The young woman stopped her activity and glanced at me. Taking in my smile and presumably failing to get the joke, she quickly looked away.

"Ma'am," I continued. "Would you mind coming to speak with me and my wife for a second?"

She scribbled a tip on her receipt, then got up and walked out of the restaurant without a backward glance.

"Quite the ladies' man," Stephanie cooed, chuckling at my expense.

"It's food for thought, at least. You know they do studies on people who take large numbers of selfies –

they're more likely to obsess over appearances, you see."

I stared at Stephanie for a moment, wondering whether she would follow me down this rabbit hole. I'd been thinking about it for weeks. It simply made sense – and I had <u>never</u> liked being photographed! I always made faces at the camera. Come to think of it, most people didn't enjoy having their picture taken. They smiled out of obligation, nothing more…

Stephanie silently stared back, causing me to wonder how many of these same thoughts were cascading through her mind. Finally, she spoke.

"It's not so much the photograph, as the coquetry it inspires."

The word was an uncommon one, and I thought to myself that she had found it in the pages of *Les Miserables*, which had been given to her last Christmas by my mother, who had asked me "Darren, what would Stephanie like for Christmas this year?" Stephanie hadn't used the word precisely correctly, but Fantine came to my mind and I understood her meaning.

"So it has that effect because she sees other peoples' reactions? Is the effect only different from a mirror in terms of audience?" I took a sip of my coffee and watched Stephanie sign the check.

Standing, we walked out of the restaurant without another word. The sun was shining brilliantly, and I reached up to the top of my head to pull down my sunglasses, fumbling only a little with them before they fell into place on my nose.

Stephanie hadn't finished with the photography thought. As we walked down the busy Austin street, the humidity of the afternoon stifled our conversational efforts only slightly more than the passerby and the traffic. I took advantage of the pause to imagine a few alternative scenarios. After all, the world was fairly weird – could cameras do something to a person's soul? Other than Stephanie's suggestion of "coquetry," I could think of no scientifically reasonable explanation.

We turned abruptly onto a deserted side street, away from the fanfare of the major thoroughfare. It was pleasantly shaded, and felt about ten degrees cooler. Birds chirped, and the din of the major avenue faded quickly as we strode in the opposite direction of it.

"Maybe it's a retroactive thing," said Stephanie.

We'd come far enough to speak quietly and be heard, but our minds had also worked as we'd walked.

"You know," she continued, "it's like a thing that changes the moment, makes you think about how it's going to be later. Or, when you look at a photo – you don't get transported to the moment it represents. You simply remember, or imagine, what it was like. The pose might be the unnatural part."

"I see," said I, loving her. "So it's only capable of doing – or stealing – anything when we're aware of it, when we stop doing whatever we were doing initially, like Schrodinger's Cat."

"Exactly!" she gushed.

I embraced her joyously, pressing a quick, but feeling, kiss onto her lips.

Sometimes, it was hard to imagine a better match for myself. No matter how strange they seemed at first, Stephanie managed to follow my thoughts – and she seemed just as entertained by them as I was.

When we reached our pot dealer's house, our conversation had shifted to small talk.

Gordon answered my knock, tattoos visible on his sleeveless arms. A former tattoo artist, he was virtually covered in them. My favorite one occurred about halfway between his wrist and his elbow, on his left arm. A circle with straight lines protruding from it in every direction, bold comic book letters proclaimed PFFFT! I'd asked him about it one day, and he said it was a tattoo of a fart.

These days, he was a technical writer at a local computer chip manufacturing company.

"Greetings," he said, welcoming us. "Ya'll having a good day?"

"Yeah, man." I considered the situation—here we were, the grown-ups. Had they always been as good as we were? As cool as we are now? I couldn't imagine it being so. I'd gotten my weed from Gordon for over twenty years, at this point.

"We had a thing going about pictures stealing people's souls, for awhile," Stephanie informed him.

"Yeah," I chimed in. "Got some sun in. Had dinner. How's your day, Gordon?"

Gordon just plopped down in his chair, motioning for the two of us to sit.

"Holy shit, guys," he chuckled, rolling his eyes. "You two have the weirdest conversations."

Stephanie smiled. "Don't look at me," she said.

END GAME

When Eddie got home for the summer, we hadn't seen him since Christmas. We lived in Houston, and he had gone to school at UT in Austin. I was in the living room, watching the U.S. Open golf tournament on TV. Janet was in the kitchen fixing herself another cup of coffee. It was Sunday, and Johnson was in the lead very late. I heard the car horn chirp as he pressed the button to lock the doors, and a few seconds later the front door swung open.

"I'm home!" Eddie said, beaming a smile.

He was wearing his gym shorts and a t-shirt in addition to his flip flops and out-of-season beanie. His suitcase sat on its side in the entry hall.

"Come here you," I said, crossing the room with my arms extended for the traditional hug.

Janet burst into the room to hug her son as well.

We ate dinner that night, and Eddie told us a little bit about the semester he'd had. I thought almost nothing of it, but when she heard he'd been in an aesthetics class, Janet offered to take him to the museum the next day. I had no choice but to tag along.

"Well, mom," Eddie was saying. "Kitsch isn't really art. It's different. Kitsch is basically pop art that becomes overcommercialized," he droned. I quit listening for a minute.

"But, Eddie," his mother broke in. "How can something that's not art be beautiful?" She paused. "Doesn't selling a work turn it into a commodity regardless of its status as kitsch or not?"

Eddie was not to be dissuaded. "Art is greater than the sum of its parts. It's communicative. The act of commissioning artwork for a specific purpose – such as a Campbell's soup can – is, in and of itself, a sort of radical de-fanging process. The company says hey, we want your art. But we want it to *mean* this particular thing. That bastardizes it, cuts off its potential value to culture."

"I see," his mother said.

I remained silent as we toured through the museum looking at this and that piece. When we reached the basement, we encountered a piece entitled 'End game'. It consisted of two skeletons and a variety of medical implements. I was impressed by it, but Eddie was far more so.

"It's profound," he shrieked. He jumped up and down a bit, grasping for words to describe his emotions.

"It's dark," his mother replied.

I put my hand on her shoulder.

"It's accurate," I chimed in. I'd been rather silent the entire trip so far, and both of them turned to look at me.

"Don't you think there's something... masturbatory... about all of this?" I asked them.

"About the art?" Janet asked.

"Why, of course, Dad!" Eddie smiled. He was thrilled that I had joined the conversation. "Art itself has no value without the culture it celebrates. Even cave drawings – pieces which were likely more functional than artistic – hold the secrets of the people and times they originated with."

I wasn't convinced.

"I'm not convinced," I said. I scratched my chin, waiting for him to elaborate. He didn't seem to have understood my point.

"Well, think about it this way: these works, for the most part, are the focal point of a conversation. This conversation is generally grounded in symbolism or aesthetics, both of which are peculiar to this or that group, place, and time. Essentially, humanity as a whole produces it all – and preserves what it deems worthy. This choice is the same as the choice between pornographic magazines: the sole purpose is to celebrate a particular aspect of an otherwise arbitrary artifact!" He paused for breath, his eyes burning. "The choice of the artifact is entirely masturbatory – self-indulgent – because it provides the beholder with an opportunity to worship herself, which it wouldn't be able to do if she didn't possess the cultural capital necessary to understand it in the first place!"

At this, I nodded.

"Which, out of all of humanity, almost no-one does or ever will!" Eddie's eyes shone with triumph.

Janet sighed, irritated with her son's support of my critical attitude.

"So," he continued, having observed our reactions, "the very act of appreciating art is simultaneously the appreciation of one's own ability to appreciate said art." He barked a short laugh. "Just as masturbation is a celebration of the fact that one has genitals and sexual desire."

I chuckled a bit. Ninety thousand dollars' worth of education had turned my son into an entertainer, that much was certain.

"Well, Eddie, what is it that makes art worth appreciating, then?"

I shouldn't have, according to the glance Janet shot me, but it was too late to take it back.

"What is it that makes masturbation worthwhile? It feels good! You look at an exhibit like this, it communicates with you, it resonates with you, and you manage to inherit what the artist wanted to impart you with: an idea." He slowed down. "The idea is what makes art beautiful, but the sexual drive one has to interact with it is what makes it masturbatory."

Janet scoffed, slightly.

"Let's go to another exhibit," I suggested. "Perhaps we'll come to something relevant."

We slowly wandered into another section of the museum, Eddie leading the way. Before long, we had reached an exhibit about abstract impressionism.

"Ah," Eddie breathed. "A Jackson Pollock."

The tremendous canvas was covered in blotches of this and that color. Pollock's genius was lost on me, but Janet certainly seemed to enjoy it.

"Do you all want to hear a story about Jackson Pollock?" Eddie inquired.

"Oh, yes," Janet said with a smile. "Isn't his work wonderful?"

I had to put a hand over my mouth to keep from laughing out loud. I'd never been a fan of abstract impressionism. Speculating about the emotion behind the man's choice to throw this or that color in this or that place was simply not my forte.

"Well," Eddie began, "Rumor has it that, in the late 1930's, J. Edgar Hoover's FBI was beginning to investigate a handful of major artists. The tactics they used were ineffective, though, until they had a breakthrough. Jackson Pollock was a lesser-known artist whose apolitical fixation upon impressionism was generally not terribly popular until the FBI began funneling moneys into art shows designed to bring popularity to his work." He broke off, quizzically looking from me to his mother.

"Well, Eddie, that sounds very interesting..." his mother said, deliberately trailing off. She probably wanted out of the conversation. I couldn't have that, though.

"So you're blaming the rise of abstract impressionism on J. Edgar Hoover?" I had to know.

"Yes, dad. Sorry, mom, I know you like the abstract impressionists. I prefer the abstract expressionists, for example, Rothko's work – but the problem is simple: Pollock's work is devoid of any meaning in itself. It doesn't symbolize anything. It symbolizes a lack of political commentary, a vacuum, perhaps. It's very ironic, given the nature of the political climate within which it arose."

He scratched his chin.

"Rothko's works are political because Rothko painted them. His views were revolutionary. We've been to the Rothko Chapel, remember?"

We all nodded together.

"Well, Pollock was basically the opposite of that. I have a friend, an artist, who maintains that Pollock's drinking problem was exacerbated by his eventual discovery of the source of his success; when he planned to re-politicize his life by going public with the news that the FBI was behind the art shows that had made his career, they ran him off the road and blamed alcohol for his death."

Janet's eyebrows arched themselves. I let out a low whistle. We were all familiar with the history of Pollock's death, but something about the story seemed to make a great deal of sense.

I was the first to speak.

"Well, that's why I dislike some of this modern stuff, then." I shrugged and turned to walk away.

Janet and Eddie followed me into the next exhibit. There was a painting, there, by Frederick Edwin Church, a romantic. It was called Heart of the Andes. After we'd taken a few moments to admire the scope and the awesome detail of the work, I broke my silence.

"What's political about this one, Eddie?" I asked, genuinely.

"This is a landscape by a Romantic era painter," he responded. "It's a celebration of the sublime scope of nature – the very idea is anti-technological," he added as an afterthought.

"What about the Mona Lisa, then?" I thought I understood but a few more examples would probably help.

"The Mona Lisa? Why, it's a study in the development of painting techniques. Perhaps it isn't the most political work that ever took place in and of itself, but think: it could be a picture of anyone. Why the mysterious woman?" Eddie began to walk, slowly, toward the exit.

"Well, I don't know. Why her?" I asked, always game.

"Well, it's simple. It's a nobleman's wife who has recently given birth. Her expression conceals joy, at having had a healthy son, and anxiety, about that young man's life. Da Vinci never thought he'd finished it, never sold it to the man who commissioned it. The artist's self-expression, his accurate rendering of the expression of the woman, was in itself so political that he could not part with the work under agreed-upon terms!" Eddie was nearly shouting as he pushed open the door and led the way into the sunlight of the Monday afternoon.

"I see!" exclaimed Janet. "Precisely what makes the painting such a statement made it impossible to employ as a means to the end of making money!"

"I suppose the masturbatory part of this is the origin of the painting?" I chimed in, expecting an emphatic agreement.

"No, Dad!"

I was surprised. I stopped walking, and I must have looked a bit puzzled. They both turned and stared at me for a moment, and Eddie took a step toward me.

"It isn't the origin of the painting: it's the sick fascination we each have with applying it to our own lives."

I shot him another puzzled glance. "How else are we to interpret it, if not from our own perspectives?"

"That's not the problem. The problem is that we've taken an accidental creation and turned it into the most popular artwork of all time!" Eddie laughed.

"After all," he got in between the chuckles, "if Da Vinci had been able to simply paint the woman with a smile on her face, it might have been the least interesting work of his career. His inability to do so perplexes us. In that face, which by all accounts was intended to show joy, we see serenity, approval, caution, depression, submission, and a definite impression of the sublime itself. The work – initially commissioned to communicate simplistic emotion – managed to capture an immense cross section of the palate of highly refined human emotional capacity! If all artists were capable of doing their jobs, all art would reach this height. That's why appreciating it so deeply is masturbatory – in order to understand why it is great, one must simultaneously acknowledge that she will never soar to such heights."

I still didn't quite follow. "So, the urge to masturbate to the Mona Lisa."

Janet laughed a bit. Eddie turned red.

"Can you appreciate a painting like that without pretending that you understand what it's like to feel that serene clash between one's mastery of emotion and the awe of the sublime awakening in you? Can you imagine Da Vinci not understanding?"

I tried, but I couldn't.

"No," I said. "We should look up pictures of the Mona Lisa online when we get home. But I definitely remember feeling a sort of otherworldly depth to the face she makes."

"That's right," said Janet. "So, Eddie, what's masturbatory about that, again?"

"You two. You're seducing yourselves into believing a bit of canvas with some paint on it is something special, and then taking more pleasure in what you create in your own minds than in what you actually experience in reality." He smiled.

Janet and I just looked at each other.

"Is there any other sort of aesthetic pleasure?" she asked.

"End game," Eddie said, matter-of-factly.

Janet and I burst out laughing. Our son was right, and he knew it.

THE GAMBLER

Flight 511 departed Dallas Fort Worth International Airport on schedule, at 11:17 AM. It was bound for Las Vegas, Nevada, and Jeremiah Southeby relished the chance to play blackjack for money only slightly more than he abhorred the concept of flying through the air in a metal tube.

The idea behind the trip was simple: Jeremy would get away for a few days, take in novel sights and sounds, try out his new card counting technique, and come home – all for less than a thousand dollars. The middle management position he had found for himself demanded nothing less than a complete change of scenery every so often, and he intended to enjoy every moment of the cut-rate vacation.

As things go, it wasn't so simple. As he arrived at the airport, he had noticed that parking was an astronomical $22/day. Then, after an hour of waiting to get through the TSA checkpoint, he was marked for a deeper search. The bomb detection registered positive, for some unknown reason, and he was condemned to what amounted to a strip search. After several minutes of invasive rubbing in a disrobed state, Jeremy was finally allowed to rush to his terminal. He had managed to arrive in time for the flight, but a cursory glance revealed that all of the aisle seats were taken. His best option was a horrifying window seat.

When the flight touched down, the woman next to Jeremy remained patiently in her seat until the rest of the cabin had finished exiting the plane. Only then did she bother to ask whether he intended to stay on board to San Jose. When Jeremy informed her that he intended to spend the weekend and the bulk of his savings in Las Vegas, she stood and allowed him to collect his bag and exit the plane.

Fuming, Jeremy walked outside to find the shuttle to his hotel. By the time he arrived, he was so irritated that his face had grown red. Jeremy stood, for a long moment, in front of the mirror in the hotel room he had booked at a substantial discount online. He sized himself up, asked himself what the problem was, and demanded that he allow himself to enjoy this weekend – whatever the cost.

The first night began with a quick elevator ride to the ground floor. The hotel where Jeremy was staying, as luck would have it, was home to a massive casino. His gambling budget was a modest $200 per night, and Jeremy intended to make that money last as long as humanly possible.

At the first table, Jeremy waited several hands to place his first bet. Since his entrance, the count was already a massive +5 and he felt he couldn't wait to get in on the action. He placed a $20 bet and was rewarded with a pair of jacks – which he split. The waitress came by, and he ordered a gin and water. The dealer dealt the first hand an ace, and the second hand saw a king. Jeremy continued winning, and drinking, in this fashion until he was up to his eyes in cash: he had already won $1300. He decided to have a bit of fun with his new $1500 nightly budget. He needed to

43

find something more entertaining before his luck ran dry.

The strip was oddly quiet, considering the number of people out and about. As he walked out of the casino, he noticed a silence that came rather unexpected. He had cashed out his chips at the window, but in the interest of making the money last, had separated the hundreds into three $500 wads and stowed each into a separate pocket. As he meandered along, taking in the sights of the Vegas strip at 1:00 AM, a dull sensation settled into Jeremy's gut. None of this was new. None of it was particularly novel. What had he come out here for, in the first place? He walked beneath a scaffold, and a prostitute approached him.

"Hey, are you looking for a good time tonight?" she asked, earnestly.

Jeremy took a moment, appraising her physique. She was quite beautiful, but he simply wasn't interested in paying for sex.

"Not that kind of good time. I'm up, and I'm not working. That's good enough for me," he replied, continuing at the same pace.

She had fallen into step with him. Her eyes lit up a bit at the news that he was up, but Jeremy had already decided not to pay too much attention to her. Jimmy Buffett's place was just up ahead, and he walked through the door without saying another word. The woman followed.

Jeremy took a seat at one of the blackjack tables, and the woman came to stand behind him. As he placed his first $100 bill on the table, he turned and got his first good look at her. She was a brunette, wearing a green dress that was covered in sequins that reflected the light. Her eye shadow was dark, but her complexion was pale and she wore her dark hair in a braid that pulled it back, out of her face, allowing her pretty cheeks and eyes to dominate the show.

"I'm Jeremy," he said, extending a hand.

"I'm Alex," she replied, taking his hand in hers.

The dealer called an abrupt end to the introduction by dealing the first set of cards. Jeremy's inexplicable lucky streak continued – the minimum bet was $20, and after an hour he had amassed another thousand dollars. He stood, gathered his chips, and walked to the window to cash out. Alex trailed him, saying nothing, but smiling as if she herself had orchestrated the winning streak.

"Well, Alex," Jeremy said as they got back out to the strip, "you're certainly not bad luck. This is as boring as work, though! What should we go do?"

"Hmm. Blackjack is a great game but the odds are pretty equal. If you want to gamble for real, you have to play craps."

Jeremy stared at her for a moment before deciding she was telling the truth. Some dice bets paid an absurd amount – and he couldn't deny that luck had played a major part in his streak, thus far.

"Where's a good place to get a game?" he asked, already visualizing himself winning at 30-to-1 odds.

"I think it's about the same wherever you go," she replied. "What about this place?"

She was pointing across the street, to the entrance of a hotel that looked even more elegant than the one where Jeremy was staying.

Jeremy pointed his elbow, allowing the woman to take hold of it, and led the way across the street. Upon entering the new casino, he noted that it appeared to be fairly empty until they arrived at the section where the dice games ran.

"I'm not sure how to do this," he explained to the woman as the dealer changed two one hundred dollar bills.

"Oh, it's easy," Alex replied, comfortably placing two of his eight twenty-five-dollar chips on the pass line. "Putting your money here means pass – if this guy rolls a seven or an eleven, you double up. If he rolls a two, a three, or a twelve, you lose. If he rolls anything else, then he establishes a point – a target he tries to hit again. If he rolls a seven before he hits the point, you lose your money. They take a bunch of other bets, too – see the numbers? You can bet on basically anything."

The shooter had rolled a seven during her brief speech, and Jeremy let the new money ride. The shooter rolled a five, and then immediately another five. The fifty-dollar bet had turned into one hundred dollars, which was now two hundred fifty dollars. Jeremy picked the money up and turned to Alex.

"That was a fast two hundred bucks. I think I like this game."

"Yeah, craps is about the most exciting thing there is. I read about an experiment once where these neuroscientists studied gambling addiction. Turns out, losing by a little is an even better high than winning. And in dice, you never seem to lose by much."

She gestured to the table. The shooter had just crapped out. The stickman was raking in all of the bets from the various numbers around the table, to a collective groan from everyone standing nearby. The odds and the payouts were foreign to Jeremy, but it seemed that the little red dice had to be making the casino money or the game wouldn't be played here. Still, the opacity of the rules probably wasn't going to work in his favor.

The two of them accepted a round of drinks from a passing waitress, and Jeremy crapped out without winning during the next few shooters – he was now in the red for the first time that evening. He decided to press his luck – placing bets on the four, the hard four, the five and the six. The shooter threw a three.

"Craps!" yelled the dealer, collecting all of the bets.

Jeremy winced as he watched his wager, $200, leave the table, but it was almost his turn to roll the dice. He placed another fifty dollars on the pass line.

The man whose turn it was to roll took an absurd amount of time in choosing which two of the five dice to roll. A fat young man in a fedora and a vest over his button-up shirt, the only impression he really conveyed in Jeremy's eyes was of someone who tries too hard. He finally settled on them, set them both on the table with the sixes facing up, and picked them up. He cradled them in his palm, rolling them around, and blew on them with the air of a magician about to pull off the trick he'd been preparing for his entire life.

Finally, he threw the dice down the table.

"Craps!" yelled the dealer.

The man winced, and stalked away from the table.

The next shooter made Jeremy $150 by hitting twice before making a point, but Jeremy picked up his winnings and held only a $50 bet on the pass line. The point, an 8, stood for long enough that Jeremy was beginning to consider placing additional bets, before the shooter's luck finally ended.

It was Jeremy's turn to roll, and Alex had disappeared. To his left, he noted, the man with the fedora had reappeared. The man was focused intently upon the dice.

"Do you want to help me pick two?" Jeremy asked, facetiously.

"I'd go for the five and the two," the man responded in all earnestness.

Jeremy picked up the five and the two, and the stickman collected the rest. Jeremy held the dice in his hand, shuffling them back and forth.

"Blow on them," the man said. "It's good luck."

Jeremy thought about making a remark about the man's poor luck earlier, but thought better of it. He blew on the dice, and threw them down the table. Two twos, or a hard four, came up.

"Good," the man said. "I'll bet on a hard six this time." He threw a twenty-five-dollar chip to the center of the table, calling his bet to the dealer.

Jeremy picked up the dice. For a moment, he hesitated. Then he pulled a one-hundred-dollar bill out of his pocket and called a bet on hard six to the dealer. The dealer, looking puzzled for a moment, changed the money and made the bet. Finally, Jeremy threw the dice.

"Hard six!" came the call.

The dealer stacked nine $100 chips next to the four $25 chips on the hard six and pushed the stack to Jeremy.

Alex reappeared, with the waitress in tow, just in time to see the pile of money being pushed toward Jeremy.

"Would you like another drink, love?" she asked, her green eyes sparkling somehow despite the dim lights.

Jeremy could have kissed her.

"Of course," he replied, magnanimously placing a $100 chip on the waitress's tray.

He turned his attention back to the table. The need to push his luck was growing stronger. He turned out his pockets - $400 from the front right, $500 from the front left. His back pocket was strangely empty, but it didn't seem to matter. He placed the $900 on the pass line with a single $100 chip.

Looking to the man to his left for approval, he chose two dice based on the fact that one had a six facing up and the other had a one, and then cupped them both in his right hand. In observance of the ceremony, he blew on them and shook them around a little bit before he threw them to the other end of the table.

"Craps!" came the call. The stick came out and raked in $1000 of Jeremy's money.

There went the down payment on a new car, Jeremy thought. There went a new iPhone. There went a plane ride to a better place than Vegas.

Alex stared in disbelief as the sum of money which could convince her to do unspeakable things disappeared into the casino's bank. She squeezed Jeremy's arm one last time, and he failed to respond. They always did that, before they quit. She knew he'd had enough of gambling for the night and that it was time to find a new mark.

Jeremy, for his part, didn't give up immediately. He placed another $50 bet on the pass line, watching the man in the fedora intently. The first roll came up a six, and he placed a large bet on the hard six. Immediately, despite having blown on the dice, he rolled a seven.

"Seven out!" the dealer yelled. The crowd around the table thinned out considerably, as people who had lost four or five or six bets opted to try a different table. Jeremy was still up a few hundred dollars, though, and decided to stick around.

"Say, man, what's your name?" he asked the man in the fedora.

"I'm Marco. You?"

"Jeremy. Do you do this a lot?"

Marco smiled.

"Yeah, man, every chance I get. I'll hit it big one of these days, quit my job. You know. That good life is out there somewhere, waiting on me."

Marco's smile was tremendous. There was something infectious about it. Jeremy asked him a few more questions, as his bankroll dwindled, but his betting was less severe than Marco's – and in the half-hour it took to lose the last $500 or so, he watched the poor bastard lose five times that.

"What do you do for work?" Jeremy asked.

"I'm a truck driver," Marco replied.

Jeremy winced. Marco had just lost what had to be several months' salary after rent and bills. He left, after that, thinking about what Alex had said.

As he walked along the strip, back to his hotel, Jeremy's mind conjured up images from his childhood. Hold the bat this way, do your hair like this. Make your resume all into one page. Try to stay in shape. Smile for the camera!

What, in all that, had gone beyond 'Blow on the dice before you roll them'?

Jeremy dined cheaply the next day and spent his time walking around instead of gambling. As hard as he tried, he couldn't think of any single piece of advice he'd ever been given that could be seen as more substantial than the gambler's tip to blow on the dice. Marco had to be making good money to be able to lose so much in the casino, but if he couldn't think of a better use for his money, how well could the poor bastard really be doing?

On the flight back to Dallas, Jeremy didn't worry about the smelly man who sat next to him. He was even content to wait a few extra minutes to disembark. He wasn't sure how it applied, yet, but the gambler had taught him something important about advice.

The Trouble with Contingency

It was just another day in the corporate world, the clerks doing their jobs were overseen by managers who were overseen by other managers and so on until you got to the very top of the ladder and started looking at CEOs and company presidents. Lukas was not the president of his company and he was not a rich investor on the board; he had a job to do and he did it well when the opportunity presented itself. Sitting there, alone in the store he was managing today, he felt a dull and aching boredom rising through his body and it felt like his soul would explode. There was nothing for it, on a slow day – most other times it was a good job.

A few hours passed lazily in the cool of the early December morning. The phone rang a few times that was all there was to it until the man with the bowtie walked into the store. On a slow day, a salesman alone in a store will do just about anything to find someone to keep him company – even a badly dressed professor works just fine. The man entered the store quietly, and even managed to browse through a few items before Lukas stood and approached him.

"Hi," he said with a grin, extending his hand by way of greeting.

"Hello, good morning," replied the man in the bowtie.

"How are you today?" Lukas asked.

"I'm phenomenal. I've just come from my final class of the semester, and I'm interested in picking up a few things for the house."

The man's cheerfulness was overwhelming. Lukas decided to go with the flow.

"Alrighty then! You've come to the right place. What kinds of things are you interested in?" he asked.

The man shrugged.

"You lead the way. I keep an open mind."

Lukas uneasily showed the professor a few pieces of furniture in the small store and arranged to have them delivered to the man's house. The ebullience the man demonstrated was out of place on this laconic hangover morning. Then, after the transaction was finished, the man did not get up to leave.

Lukas sat there in his office chair for a long moment, silently contemplating the man.

"So, Lukas, do you know what the meaning of life is?" piped up the professor.

"That one's beyond me. I don't even know where to begin," Lukas shrugged, feeling torn between the desire to get the eccentric man out of his store and the quest for entertainment on a boring day.

"Well you get that a lot, asking people the questions I like to ask them." The man sat back in his chair, calmly contemplating Lukas from a slightly increased distance. "Really, there isn't that much to it. Do you want to know the meaning of life?"

"Of course, I do. But you aren't going to tell me. You're going to give me some kind of random spiel about your opinion or try to convert me to some weird religion or something, aren't you?" Lukas stood up, preparing to usher the man to the door.

The professor said nothing, but continued to sit across the desk from Lukas, staring at him in a manner that bordered upon being concerned and simultaneously conveyed a somewhat hostile attitude. After a moment went by without Lukas sitting back down, he shrugged and pushed himself up, using the leather bound armrests of the wooden chair.

"People pay good money for a chance to talk to me like this. I'm willing to give it to you for free because I like you and I can tell by your product demonstration that this isn't exactly your calling in life."

"What if it's not? Are you saying I'm bad at my job? I don't care." Lukas shrugged, feeling unnerved by the man's expression.

"Exactly. Lukas, do you know why you don't care? Do you know why this isn't your calling?" The man felt he had found a nerve, but Lukas disagreed.

"It's just a job. Its only purpose is to pay the bills." *Why else would I be here? It sure isn't for my health,* Lukas thought to himself, beginning to march the man to the entrance of the store.

"Are you educated?" the man asked. He hadn't moved.

Lukas turned to face the professor, shrugging again.

"Yes, but I studied marketing. Philosophy is too weird. No use for that kind of crap." Somehow, Lukas knew that his words wouldn't offend this man.

Upon hearing that Lukas had a bit of experience with philosophy, and didn't like it, the professor smiled and took a step forward. He put his hand on Lukas' shoulder.

"Well, then, you probably already know what I'm going to tell you. The meaning of life, for you, right now, is dissatisfaction. There isn't anything you're happy with because every day you come to work and do your best to make someone else money. You make money too, but if you had your own business you'd make more. That's the secret to the meaning of life – it is contingent upon the moment and the circumstances that pertain to the specific incidence of life in question."

The man smiled, clearly waiting for a response.

Lukas stood patiently, not understanding.

"I'm sure I'll find my calling somehow," he said.

The professor was not surprised by this response. Lukas could feel his posture changing as the man's cool demeanor wore down his last line of sarcastic defenses.

"Lukas, you aren't listening to me. Your calling is to be you every moment of your life – it is your destiny and it is unavoidable."

"Who am I though? What does that mean?"

The questions continued in his head, but Lukas managed to cut off the flow. A woman walked into the store, a few feet away. Lukas noted her arrival, but did not turn away from his conversation.

"Ah, we're getting to an interesting place. Do you see how I'm dressed?" The man spread his arms, gesturing to his dated suit and polka-dot bowtie.

Lukas chuckled. "Badly?"

"Yes," the man chuckled, "but do you know why?"

"Why?"

"Because it's me, Lukas. I'm the guy who dresses badly and has strange conversations with people who aren't particularly interested. I'm Professor Rudolph Butler. Who are you?" Lukas had gotten the man's name during the sale, but somehow hearing the title with it lent an unexpected air of status to him now.

"I'm a young man looking for something to do with myself. I'm happy enough with the people around me but if I could just figure out what I'm supposed to do…" he made a gesture of futility with his hands. The professor nodded. "I want to be happy. I like my life but it doesn't fill me up, I guess you might say." Lukas was struggling, but he could feel his own urgent need to have this conversation. It felt right, somehow.

"You don't have to do it alone and you don't have to do it today. These things take time."

The professor turned toward the door, gesturing to the woman, and Lukas hesitated.

"Don't be shy, Lukas. I'm about to leave. Do you have something to ask me?"

"What can I do to find out who I am?"

"Ah, well who am I to answer that question?"

Lukas frowned.

"I suppose the best advice I could give would be something like this: be good to those around you and try to get what you can out of the lessons your life has to teach you."

With those words, the professor turned and was out the door before Lukas could respond.

Lukas thought about the conversation, wishing he had been able to get more out of the brief words of the professor. He imagined himself in the future: *'What can I do?' he thought, over and over. It became a sort of mantra for panic attacks that would plague him for a long time after that day. It was sometimes followed by 'now' or 'about this' but many times it was the simple question that plagued his thoughts and followed him, haunting him, for years to come. There had been an answer, and he hadn't captured it, and that fact chewed the pit of his stomach every day and every night.* No. That wasn't right.

"Excuse me, Professor!" he exclaimed, poking his head out the door. "Do you have a few minutes more? We could go get a coffee, or a beer, or something. I don't want this conversation to end yet," he explained.

The professor turned, smiling. His forehead was mildly creased, Lukas noted, and his green eyes sparkled with a new warmth. The white hair that curled into an amorphous blob atop his head matched the beginnings of the beard that manifested itself as stubble upon his face, and he had a dimple to the left of his wide grin which caught a bit of a shadow in the mid-morning sun.

"Of course," he said.

Lukas took a moment to usher the baffled woman out of the store before he locked the door and walked with the professor to a bar down the street. Once the waitress had brought a pair of beers to them, the professor began asking questions again.

"So, Lukas, thank you for the beer. I suppose I need to know what you're interested in hearing from me?" He pronounced the statement as a question, masterfully forcing the ball into Lukas' court.

"Ehrm. Um. Yes," Lukas stammered for a moment.

"Well, perhaps we should start with something that interests you."

Lukas gazed at the ceiling tiles for a moment, then looked out the window. There was a sun shining down on the trees, the grass, and the sidewalk. A few people walked by, and more sat in their cars waiting for the light to turn green.

"Well, what about that old riddle? If a tree falls in the forest, and nobody's around to hear it, does it make a sound?" He chuckled a bit, amused that even when he was this interested in a conversation he couldn't think of anything better to lead with.

"Ahh. Haha," said the professor. "Well, I suppose we can talk about that just as easily as anything else." He took a moment to clear his throat. "A lot of times, philosophy seems overbearing – but that's usually something contextual about it. It gets used for a different end than the mere pursuit of knowledge. Really, all philosophy itself is, is a method of questioning – an interrogative exploration of meaning. I'll show you how it works."

The professor paused for a moment, but Lukas was speechless. He watched the man take a long drink of beer, and lifted his own glass as a sort of afterthought.

"If a tree falls in the forest, and nobody is around to hear, does it make a sound? It's a cliché. And it seems trivial, at first glance. The question is a *koan*, a riddle without an answer. Buddhist monks used to use these to meditate upon as they sought to develop their minds. So, let's have a look. Empirical means are the investigative techniques scientists rely upon. It's safe to say that our question bars them from being used in

59

the answer – after all, observation of any sort will involve someone being around to hear somehow. The real question, then, is something like this: Does the sound we hear when a tree falls exist independently of us? Most people admit that they don't know, upon reflection, and nobody can really claim to be able to find out. Why is it interesting to meditate upon, then?"

It took a moment for Lukas to realize that this question wasn't rhetorical.

"Um, well, I – I guess it's just a quick glance at the question. What do you think?"

The professor chuckled, finished his beer, and continued.

"When we analyze the problem more carefully, it becomes clear that it is impossible to say that the tree makes a sound if nobody is around to hear. The reason why, is simple: the sound has two parts. The first part is the set of vibrations that seem to be caused by the tree's impact with its environment, and the second is the listener's interpretation. It is impossible to call something a sound without there being someone to hear it because the concept of sound implies a listener; this listener thus plays a fundamental role. What do you think about that?"

"I can see your point. I guess I think the vibrations must have more to them than that. But there really isn't a way – without observing them or their effects somehow – to argue that point! Interesting stuff!"

Lukas' voice was getting a bit louder, and when the waitress stopped by to offer them another round he felt a bit embarrassed. But this was fun! Of course he'd buy another round.

"Thanks, Lukas. I guess to sum it up we could say that to contemplate a sound that is not heard is impossible because the act of hearing is part of the creation of the sound – it is what you might call a necessary condition. We tend to assume that the sound has some sort of being of its own, independent of us, and this yields a paradox that I like to think of as the trap of language. Concepts like perfection and independent truth seem quite vacuous upon further examination, because they're simply in our heads. Without us, the observers, there can be no such thing as a perfect widget or a truth that exists without being called a truth."

Lukas remained quite spellbound. He began to wonder how it was that he had ever successfully communicated anything at all.

"We're at a crossroads, Lukas. It will take awhile, but I can explain what I mean a bit further. I've been reading a lot of Heidegger lately but to be quite honest I can't seem to manage to publish any of the things I'm about to tell you. Do you know what recursion is?"

The man lifted his glass to his lips and patiently waited as Lukas invented a definition he thought would be acceptable.

"I remember it coming up during math. I think a recursive function is one that can modify itself?"

"Indeed it is. Well, language is like that. The mere act of naming or labelling has a quite complicated impact upon our understanding of the thing thus named. My favorite instance of this is the problem Heidegger invented *dasein* as a solution to. Heidegger differentiated between being-in-the-world as humans

61

do, and as other things do. While it may be problematic – many contemporary philosophers such as Galen Strawson discuss concepts like panpsychism, or the idea of a conscious universe – it does show us something interesting about language. Any time we talk about Being, we're only capable of talking about aspects of it that are known and talked about – so you might say that our language can only reach something you might call *being-analyzed.*"

Lukas looked up to see the waitress coming back, and nodded to her for another round. The professor sat, silently gazing at him, for another minute or two before he finally admitted that this was going over his head.

"Well, it's a difficult thing to explain. The fault is more with me than with you. I guess I can backtrack a bit to see if you catch up. What I like to call the *trap of language* is a paradox that we tend to assume the falsity of. The problem is this: people overlook the contingency of the things that they say upon the context in which they say them. In some sense, by listening to my words, you're creating a version of the conceptual model I'm attempting to relay to you. I'm providing you with a schema, and nothing more. However, though I might contain all of this information in my mind, the argument is not complete until you manage to understand it – you have to recreate it in order for us to say that I successfully communicated it to you. This leaves us in a precarious position because it renders my success in arguing this point contingent upon your adequately interpreting, applying, and understanding it."

"I think I'm beginning to follow. Can you give me another example?"

"Let's take the famous nature/nurture debate from psychology. Which do you think is more crucial to the development of a particular person's personality?"

Lukas had studied this during an introduction to psychology class, years ago, and couldn't remember precisely which answer was correct.

"I suppose nature. After all, genetics are very powerful."

"I can appreciate that point. But think of it this way: if you have a particular personality at birth, as the nature hypothesis would have to maintain in order to remain internally consistent, then wouldn't you also have to know yourself from an early age? After all, if nature contains every aspect of what you'll be and your environment has no part in it – which I know is unlikely to be your stance – then how could you not know you'd spend six months or a year selling furniture in your 20's? No, this investigation of what we might call the 'hard' nature thesis shows that nurture must have an equal part to play. Our reactions to our environment shape what we do, and what we do shapes who we become."

"Ahhh. I see. Yes, I understand that. How does it relate to our topic, though?" Lukas felt excited. Seeing these concepts come together was somehow almost magical to him.

"Well, that's precisely how the language works. It is used to say something that seems to imply the falsity of its opposite, but rarely are things so cut and dried. A philosopher named Hegel talked about the dialectic – a Greek word meaning something along

63

the lines of through the thought process. His method was later simplified to something along these lines: good thinking, or good communication, is a process consisting of thesis, antithesis, and synthesis. First you state your point, then you state a counterpoint, and then you state your point again while taking the argument against it into account."

"So that's how to avoid the trap of language? You have to use the dialectic?"

"To put it simply, yes." The professor shrugged. "Interesting, isn't it?"

"Yeah. And it sounds like a sales mechanism we use – feature, advantage, benefit. They come in threes. You never just tell someone what something is; you have to tell them what it does for them. And more than once."

The professor chuckled. "I worked in sales once."

"Were you any good?"

"Not really. I went to grad school to get away from it."

"How's the professor gig?"

"Well, it's not great. The jobs are very competitive."

"Do you work at the university?"

The professor sighed. "I wanted to. I thought I had the potential to do quality research, to publish, to live the academic life. Instead, I had kids. I love them, but the work I do is mainly administrative. I had to take a community college job instead of adjuncting at a bigger school so that they could grow up with state benefits. Maybe one of these days I'll catch a break, but I can't afford to be an adjunct." He took a long drink of beer.

"Well, I'm sorry to hear it's so hard. Drinks are on me!" Lukas raised his glass.

The professor smiled, raising his own glass. "To contingency!"

CONVINCING PEOPLE

Travel is an integral part of the business world. Air travel, in particular, saves firms millions of dollars each year by allowing them to offer face-to-face product support around the country. Investors have contributed millions of dollars to fund these operations in return for a large share of the profits made by companies which are able to operate an industry in a large-scale territory at a fraction of the cost implied in a storefront.

Bill Donahue was a corporate sales rep for just such a company, but he wasn't allowed to take his gun when he travelled. His home state was Texas, and it was very comforting to him to consider the consequences someone would incur by attempting to rob and/or murder him there. Not a true coward, but a news-minded one, Bill travelled frequently for work. He supported territories in Louisiana, Oklahoma, and northern and eastern Texas.

Jimmy grinned throughout the conversation. He had a distinctive tattoo, a rainbow-colored E inside of a circle, that had started it. Bill hadn't known what it meant, and after a cursory explanation, Jimmy had asked him what he did for a living. It was impressive, and Jimmy found himself wondering why he wasn't able to work on the corporate circuit – he'd gotten himself a degree, but there didn't seem to be any jobs open. Working in the Royal Pub, he enjoyed meeting all of the travelers that came through but it was a very slow afternoon.

"Well Bill, it sounds like they keep you fairly busy. I suppose that's good at least," he shrugged, polishing a glass. "It beats working here, I'd bet you make a lot of money."

"Sure, Jimmy. It really isn't bad. Do you mind putting on the news?" Bill took a long drink of beer, and leaned back in his chair. His eyes didn't leave the screen for several minutes.

Jimmy kept washing dishes until he noticed the suit's glass had reached a very low level.

"Can I get you another Shiner?" he asked.

"Sure thing, Jimmy. Do you want to take a shot of whiskey with me?"

"Well I don't see why not," Jimmy replied, pouring.

Just then, a news story began. Seventeen dead, forty injured. AR-15, crazy guy, crowded concert.

"What a damn shame," Bill began.

Jimmy had finished pouring, and he slid the beer and a small glass of whiskey over toward Bill.

"What's that?" he asked, turning to look up at the TV screen. "Oh fuck me. Another goddamned shooting?"

"Yeah. You know, I think they ought to allow people at concerts to carry concealed weapons. We'd see a lot less of this kind of shit, you know?" Bill reached out, picking up his glass of whiskey.

Jimmy raised his glass, letting Bill follow suit.

"To protecting ourselves and our families," Bill muttered.

Jimmy slammed the whiskey, plunking the little glass onto the bar mat upside down.

"You know, I think it's bullshit."

"What's that, Jimmy? People shooting everybody up?" Bill wanted to know. He finished the little glass of whiskey and reached for the beer to wash away the harsh taste of the liquor.

"No, Bill. I think guns ought to be illegal. I sure as hell wouldn't want one in here. I keep a baseball bat behind the bar in case I have to chase someone out, but people start bringing guns around right before they start shooting each other. I don't make enough to put myself in harm's way like that." Jimmy poured each of them another drink.

"Here's to keeping guns illegal," he said.

Bill didn't reach for the drink. "Thanks," he said, "but I need to pace myself a little bit more. Why the hell don't you have a gun back there? Aren't you worried about getting robbed?"

"Bill, I have insurance for that. There isn't a single fucking thing in here I can't live without if there's a problem like that – if I start getting robbers in here, it's a sure sign I need to find something else to do anyway."

"But what if they shoot you?"

"Then they shoot me. I'll take my fucking chances. The crazies won't go away, but I'd feel like a real arsehole if I turned my back and someone got my own gun to shoot me with? I think the whole issue is fairly fucking stupid," he said. "The news has another mass shooting every day, and the conceal to carry guys never seem to do a fucking thing about it even when they're nearby!"

"I like to think my chances would be a little better," Bill began.

Jimmy picked up the shot he had poured for Bill and drank it.

"I don't think they would. How would you like to live in Africa, or Mexico? You could be a body guard for the cartel or something if you like guns so fucking much. Might even make more money!" Jimmy couldn't keep the dismissive attitude out of his voice. He knew he should keep a lid on it in front of the customers, but enough was enough.

"I appreciate you opening up to me like this, but I can't believe you don't think one decently-trained guy with a pistol could have taken that guy out."

"If he sees a guy with a drawn gun, he probably just shoots that guy first. I really don't think a conceal to carry guy would have done anything except secure himself a quicker death. Besides, when that actually does happen, the handgun guys always keep them holstered because they don't want to end up in a shootout with the police."

Bill shook his head.

"You're missing the point. What if *everybody* had a concealed pistol ready to go?"

Jimmy shrugged. "Then all someone would need would be a pistol. Shoot this guy, shoot that guy, soon enough everyone's shooting each other because they can't tell each other apart."

Bill took a long drink of beer.

"The safest thing is to make sure that the crazy fucks who decide to shoot everybody up can't get guns before the rest of us find out they've snapped," Jimmy finished.

"I guess that makes sense. Was this one a crazy or one of those Islamics?"

"I think even the guys who join the terror groups have mental illnesses man. I don't think a sane person does that kind of shit. The concept of wanting to.. what? Take over? Just fuck everything up? Scare everyone? I don't think they really have any fucking idea what they're doing. They're really not all that good at it. Take their guns away, and you get what? A guy who snaps and tries to make a bomb? Good luck. These assholes don't have the IQ for that shit."

Bill listened intently, watching as Jimmy poured two more whiskeys as he spoke.

"Well, I guess that makes sense. I'm a homeowner, though, in a fairly nice neighborhood. I like to think I'd be able to handle it if someone broke into my house," he mused.

"Sure. And I think having a shotgun somewhere in the house where you can get to it, but your kids can't, is probably a good idea – but nobody's ever really even tried to say that's a bad thing to do. A shotgun or a 30.06 ought to make enough noise and be powerful enough to stop anybody who shows up to cause trouble. Doesn't mean you need an assault weapon or grenade launcher."

"Yeah, and I'm not one of those guys who think the government is gonna come for 'em one of these days. Hell, I couldn't stop the US Army if they decided to come get me. No such thing as zombies. I guess we agree about the assault weapons." Bill shrugged and downed the shot of whiskey.

"Do you like the NRA?" Jimmy asked, genuinely interested. His Mohawk stood up straight and his knuckles had tattoos that spelled out the words *Foul Play* but Bill was finding that he made a lot of sense.

The question landed on deaf ears, nonetheless.

"Fuck, man, Obama'd be taking my shotgun away if I didn't," he said.

"Dude. No. Bill. If you really think that, you're crazy. Under Clinton, they passed a bill – 80% or so of Americans supported it. Then, Bush and the Republicans let it expire in 2004. Since then, the rate of mass shootings has skyrocketed." Jimmy pulled the bottle back out. He could feel himself becoming more heated, but it didn't matter. Bill would be a good tipper – he wasn't getting offended.

"Well, I guess that makes sense. But was that really the NRA's fault?"

"Yeah, Bush was real close to them. So are a lot of the congressmen. You know, there are some guys who say that the NRA is actually closer to ISIL than to average Americans like us – they basically arm all the potential domestic terrorists and make sure the politicians look the other way. Then it's all so tragic when some idiot snaps and kills a bunch of people, but of course we don't cut off the supply of guns. The way I have it figured, if you're normal until you snap, you won't break the law to buy a gun. Somebody's gonna notice your behavior if you're breaking the law and maybe even be able to help you out before it comes to that..." he trailed off.

Bill's face was incredulous.

"Wait, are you really trying to compare the NRA to ISIL?" he blurted.

"Yeah, for all I fucking know they're in league with one another. There's no way we're safer with all the assault weapons out there – and there's no way the ISIL guys have any real plans either. Maybe they're all making money off the US gun market together or some shit like that," Jimmy trailed off again, watching Bill react to the message.

"Well, fuck. I guess I don't really know what the hell to say about that. I gotta get the fuck out of here, man, but you've given me a lot to think about."

Jimmy swiped the card and left the receipt in front of Bill without charging him for any of the shots. The bottle they'd killed had cost him about $20, but he'd had about half or more of it himself. When he looked at the tip Bill had left him, he realized he'd actually still made money off the deal – the tip was $35.

Bill waved from the door, then walked out into the Oregon night. He went back to his hotel, intent upon taking a shower and looking up some of the points Jimmy had made during their discussion, but passed out instead. He had an early flight the next day. When his cousin, Darren met him at the airport back in Texas, the two of them discussed the shooting.

"God wouldn't have let this happen if those people hadn't been sinning," was the major point Darren wanted to make. Bill sighed and nodded with agreement – it was just easier to let people say what they wanted to. Plus, he didn't want to run the risk of getting into some shitty argument with his cousin.

FOR WANT OF ADVENTURE

Sometimes, it's all you can do to hold it together. James stood in the glow of the halogen lights, a whiskey bottle in one hand, empty. His blood pressure was high, his face was red, and he could not understand why he was here. He took another deep swig of Jameson. He did not belong in Prague. His stomach hung over the top of his belt. He had had money, once. Money and a home—a boring life, back in the states, but he had thrown it all away for want of adventure.

That morning, something had felt... off. James could not remember what had come over him, that day, as he smashed the hotel bathroom mirror with the whiskey bottle. As he slumped to the floor in cardiac arrest, his mind drifted back to the last day of his old job and to the end of his old life.

It had been a normal day, aside from the deep feeling that something was wrong in the pit of his stomach. He had walked into the office, holding the thermos of coffee he always brought with him from the house.

Half an hour later, Mrs. Lambert came in.

"How do you do today, Cecelia?" he asked.

"I'm in a sorry state, Doctor. I tried what you suggested last week. When Edward came home from work, angry as usual, I smiled and acted upbeat. Eventually, though, his pessimism beat me down again. I still think about killing myself after a few hours of his company." She frowned, snatched a Kleenex from the box near the sofa, and began to cry. "I don't know how it's come to this! I hate this life."

"Now, Cecelia, what real reason do you have to be sad?" Dr. James McElroy leaned forward in the plush armchair over his crossed legs, his voice soothing, as the woman on the couch continued to weep.

"You were supportive, you were helpful. You cannot control your husband's mind, and you aren't responsible for his temperament." He nodded as she set the tissue aside.

One last sniff, and the crying had finished.

"Good. We talked about this last week – you need to manage *your* emotions. You can't hold yourself responsible for *his*."

"Doctor," she began, averting her eyes. She sat up straighter. "I want to try something new. Anything we do here is confidential, right?" With that, she looked into the therapist's eyes meaningfully.

"Of course, Cecelia," he replied.

"Come over here." She patted the couch instructively.

James got up and took a seat next to the beautifully mature blonde woman. She stood, unbuttoning her blouse. She leaned in, placing an expert kiss on his clean-shaven cheek.

"Maybe if we fuck I'll feel better about my marriage."

James put his hands on her hips, met her eyes with his. The two of them gazed at each other for a long moment, then her hands began to unbuckle his belt. She pushed her lips onto his.

"You're a beautiful woman," said James, between kisses.

Cecelia rolled onto the couch, pulling James on top of her. She hiked up her skirt, still kissing him. When he entered her, she moaned beautifully.

Several minutes later, James was re-buckling his belt. She was still getting dressed, but it was time for the next appointment to begin. As Cecelia tossed her hair, managing to tame its disorder almost as if by magic, James cleared his throat.

"Same time next week?" he asked.

"Yes. Doctor, I feel wonderful." She picked up her purse, smiling at him.

"I'm glad," said James, sitting back down in the armchair. He picked up his notepad and pen and flipped to a clean page as the Henderson kid walked in to take Cecelia's place on the couch.

"Hello, Jonathan," said James, crossing his right leg over his left.

"Mornin' doc." Jonathan was too skinny to be athletic, and the unruly mop of his hair was largely hidden by a flat-brim Colorado Rockies cap. James immediately sensed an above-average intellect behind the kid's blue eyes.

"What brings you to my office, Jonathan?"

Jonathan shrugged, leaning forward. He stared at the coffee table for a long moment before breaking his silence. The initial phase of the interview took about ten minutes, and James easily reached a diagnosis. The kid suffered from ADHD and was probably bipolar type B. These were both rather common maladies for intelligent young people who didn't readily fall into place, and James had to restrain

75

himself from trying to persuade the young man to go to medical school.

"Doc, I enjoyed this little talk but I have a question for you before our time is up."

James sat up a bit straighter, wondering what would come next.

"I'm sick of always being a different person every day. The guy I am today is here because the guy I was last week had a strange conversation with his mother. Today, I feel pretty good," Jonathan said, fidgeting. "But the guy I was last week felt lousy. Why do things change so often?"

Yes, definitely type B bipolar. Maybe the kid was schizophrenic as well.

"That's interesting. Do you hear voices?"

"Haha. No. I'm sane enough, I guess. I'm mostly just sick of all the bullshit going on in this crazy, mixed-up world. I feel like I don't really fit anywhere, you know?" The kid had taken out his car key, one of those squares that had a button on it you could press to release, and was now playing with it. He would press the button, catch the key with his finger, and push it back into the folded position.

James watched a few cycles of this, growing annoyed.

"The world seems reasonable enough to me," he replied. "We reap what we sow."

"Doc, you know I'm a different person in here than I am out there, right?"

James smiled at this. Perhaps this kid was someone he could help after all.

"Yes, of course! You're affected by your surroundings. We all are."

"I'm here because the out-there guy isn't happy. He's alternatively pissed off and depressed because he isn't in control of his life. The world is chaos, and there he is in the middle of it. He just wants to get by, but it seems pointless – he can't catch a break." Jonathan was still clicking the key and pushing it back, staring at the ceiling as his words rolled out.

There, James thought. He had opened up.

"Jonathan, I mean no disrespect. But you're communicating signs of depression, and I have to ask. Do you intend to hurt yourself?"

"Haha," Jonathan said. "Of course I don't. I just want two plus two to equal four, if you know what I mean." He put the keys in his pocket and sat up straight again.

Interested, James clicked his pen and wrote the word 'Philosopher' on the yellow legal pad on his lap. He took a quick glance at the clock, then flipped to a clean page and wrote 2+2=4. He set the pad down on the coffee table and put the pen on top of it.

"There you go," he said.

Jonathan picked up the pen and drew a line through the equal sign.

"Math has nothing to do with it, doc. I drink. I smoke. I can't give up either. This me, in front of you today, is an addict because some other guy, years ago, picked up bad habits." He slouched, evidently feeling depressed or powerless.

James thought for a minute, reclaiming his notepad from the table.

"Yes. So you see, two plus two does equal four after all. What you just described is order, not chaos.

You're feeling bad because you want to change your behavior but you can't do it retroactively."

James smiled as the kid gathered his thoughts. About five minutes remained, the clock said.

Jonathan stood up. He began to pace.

"Doc, you're wrong. I feel bad because I can't go to sleep tonight and wake up tomorrow. Every day, I have a different personality. Even if you make a leap of faith, assume the continuity of the transcendental I between now and then, it still doesn't work. It isn't that I'm suicidal, it's that I want to quit dying each night when I go to sleep. I want to live."

The kid had stopped pacing, and now stood with his hand on his chin, staring at the doctor from a few feet away.

"Well, Jonathan, I understand you're going through a lot. However, it's noon and we've finished our session for today. Would you like to continue this next week?" James set the notepad on the table as he spoke, standing up to escort his patient to the door.

"I won't be here next week."

"Yes you will, Jonathan. Of course you will. We all will, except those of us who die. I appreciate your philosophical acumen but matters of practice demand a certain... practicality." He pulled the door open, gesturing for Jonathan to lead the way into the hall. "And if you can't agree with that, try to enjoy each new rebirth. Try to enjoy your life, and be content with doing the best you can."

Jonathan nodded, looking pensive as he crossed the waiting area and left the office. James plucked his coat from the rack behind the receptionist's desk and waved to her as he left for lunch.

THE HOMECOMING

The next day was Friday, and James took the day off work. He flew to Chicago for a conference that lasted all weekend, settling for the last flight home on Sunday night. Melissa picked him up from the airport in her Range Rover.

"Hello, darling," James said as he took the passenger's seat. He leaned in to kiss his wife of seven years. "You're beautiful," he said.

Melissa put the car into drive, smiling thinly. The rest of the drive was conducted largely in silence, leading James to wonder what had happened. Did Melissa know what he'd been doing? He loved her very much, but something had changed. Perhaps she had discovered some sort of evidence of his recent sexual adventures with other women.

"James," she said, as the garage door rattled its way back down. "I have to tell you something." She faced him, looking him in the eye, there in front of the door into the kitchen.

James found his eyes unable to hold her stare. He waited, staring at the concrete of the garage floor.

"I'm leaving," she said.

James was unable to reply. He did manage to make eye contact with her, though.

She choked back a sob. Had she found out about the cheating?

"I'm leaving," she repeated.

James held his breath and looked away. Maybe if he let her vent, this would pass.

"I need someone with more life. I need more adventure. You're the same every day and you make

79

me the same and it's secure, it's stable, it's really wonderful, but I hate it." Tears streamed freely down her face.

"Melissa," he began, before he thought better of it. "Let's go inside." He pushed the door open and led the way to the living room. This bought him a moment to think about what he was going to say. All of a sudden, he understood. She'd changed. He knew she would, everyone did eventually. It was fine.

"Don't you have anything to say?" she asked.

He had been silent about this for too long already. Panic began to reach him through the shock. There was nothing for it but the truth.

"Melissa, I know how you feel," he said, sitting down on the expensive couch. "Thursday I had a patient. He said he was a different person every day. I didn't really believe him, I guess. But it stuck with me. I think he was right, Melissa. I think you're right. Do you want a divorce?"

Melissa took a seat next to him, reached for his hand, finding it with hers.

"I want adventure, James. Can you help me with that? I don't hate you, I just can't stand this vanilla life anymore!" She began to sob again.

James wrapped his arms around the woman he loved. She buried her face in his shoulder, and he gave her a long squeeze. Suddenly, he stood up. He walked to the kitchen, poured himself a glass of whiskey over ice.

"Do you want a drink, Melissa?" he called.

"I'd love a gin and water," came the reply.

James made his way back to the living room with a drink in each hand.

"We have love, but not novelty," he began.

Melissa nodded agreement.

"You're leaving if I don't provide it. Maybe you'll leave anyway. I can't control you, and I don't want to. I thought this life would give us peace, strength, and happiness... but I suppose I was wrong." James let out a sigh.

"Yes, James." Melissa was quite cool, suddenly. "I need to live, not to survive. I'm glad for our love, but it isn't enough anymore. I need fresh air."

"You realize how crazy this sounds? I make a fucking living dealing with headcases who say things like that!"

James had finished his drink, and he smashed the glass on the floor in his sudden rage. It was as if something inside had snapped. Seven years of repressed fury flooded into the present as he crossed to the living room wall where his diploma hung in its glass frame. He tore it from the wall, hurling it into the unlit fireplace.

Melissa, who had frozen at the uncharacteristic outburst, smashed her glass on the hardwood floor too, a wordless cry escaping her lips. She tore a lamp from the end table and hurled it through the plate glass window and into the back yard. Her eyes found the flatscreen TV and she seized a barstool from the island in the kitchen, marching back across the living room to wreak destruction upon it.

James snatched her car keys and ran into the garage. He put the car into gear without opening the garage door and floored the accelerator. The Range Rover roared as it lurched into motion with a squeal of tires and launched itself through the back wall of the garage. The refrigerator skidded across the room on its side as the car continued into the island, where it finally high-centered. Water spewed from a broken pipe as James got out of the vehicle.

Melissa walked back into the kitchen, and James wrapped his arms around her. Smiles lit up both of their faces as James slung his wife over his shoulder and carried her into the bedroom.

Afterward, the two got dressed and James led Melissa into the garage. His Audi roadster was still in working order.

"Want to go get a tattoo?" he asked, putting the car into reverse.

"Yes."

Tires squealed as James floored the accelerator, backing the car out through the garage door. When they got to the street, he put it into drive and made it downtown in what must have been record time. He got a skull and crossbones tattooed on his back and Melissa had 'Stay Calm' done across her knuckles.

THE DIVORCE

After the tattoos were completed, James and Melissa had a few drinks at a local bar. They decided to go home and have sex again, but when they arrived there were police cars and fire trucks outside their house. James made a quick U-turn and drove to the airport. It was still early enough to catch a flight out of town.

As he purchased tickets, Melissa had a drink at the bar. Life was already beginning to feel fresh and new again.

He held out two tickets, facedown, when he took the seat next to his wife at the bar.

"Pick your poison, honey," he said. "One is to Paris, and the other is to Cancun."

"Beautiful," said Melissa .

She chose the ticket from his left hand, then gave him a quick kiss. The two boarded separate planes, carrying only the clothes on their backs and the smiles on their faces.

THE MONSTER WEARS MAKE-UP

Seated on a bench in the mall, Penelope watched the Saturday crowds rush past. There was something magical about being idle in the midst of such madness. A trancelike sedation overtook her senses, and she managed to reach a quasi-meditative state of thoughtlessness. Each passing human body had a goal, but Penelope didn't even have an identity.

A boy skipped by, laughing. He made eye contact with the woman on the bench, waved without thinking about it, and turned to look over his shoulder. Seeing something, he broke into a run, disappeared into the crowd of people. Penelope turned her attention back to the area directly in front of her bench, hoping to catch a glimpse of whoever might be chasing him. One of the faces was familiar!

Daphne met Penelope's eyes with her own frigid green stare. Her face broke into a grin, and the frustration that had resided there moments ago all but disappeared.

"Penelope?! Oh my god!"

Penelope fought to keep herself from wilting. Daphne was an old high school acquaintance. Her shrill voice had pierced the moment and the sight of her face ripped Penelope's spirit out of anonymity to jam it back into her life. Penelope stood, quickly, extending her arms to embrace the woman.

"Daphne!"

"Hah! How many years has it been? Oh, it's so good to see you, I didn't realize you'd moved here!"

The two women sat down on the bench, Daphne laughing and Penelope steeling herself against the storm to come.

"Oh my goodness," she said by way of diversion, picking up Daphne's left hand. "It's beautiful! When did you get married?"

"Oh, I married Jake about ten years ago. Our spawn escaped earlier and I was actually chasing him when I ran into you! What are you doing all the way out here?"

Something wasn't right about Daphne, Penelope thought. The smile, the stare, the raised eyebrows. It was all just so unsettling.

"Well, I'm an artist. I work at the Italian place across town and sometimes I like to come watch the people. You know, to get ideas about things to paint." Penelope smiled broadly, thinking of the work she enjoyed.

"You're a painter? That's fantastic. I'd love to see your work, is it for sale anywhere?"

"Well, no, I'm still not through making it happen yet," Penelope said carefully.

Just then, a crash diverted Daphne's attention. There was something reptilian about this woman, Penelope thought. The years of tanning had rendered her skin prematurely leathery, and perhaps there was a hint of Botox?

A man screamed something, and Penelope turned to see what she was staring at. The boy from earlier was a deep shade of red, with his hands clasped behind his back. An enormous stack of shoeboxes had fallen; shoes and boxes now littered the aisle. Daphne stood, rapidly covering the distance to her troublemaking child with angry strides.

"Peter!" she screamed. The boy looked up, terrified. "Come here, you little brat!"

Peter winced as she took him by the earlobe, jerking him toward her.

"Lady," the shoe store clerk began, moving his hands in a gesture toward the mess. "You need to teach that little bastard some manners." At this, he angrily pointed a finger at Peter.

Daphne was unfazed. She gave Peter a shove, and turned to follow him back to the bench where Penelope waited.

"Whatever," she yelled over her shoulder. "You look almost forty and you work in a mall. You're the last person I'm going to be taking advice from."

The man's face turned red. He opened his mouth, and closed it. He turned around and began to pick up the mess.

Daphne pushed Peter onto the bench next to Penelope, taking a moment to observe her victim at work.

"Sorry son of a bitch," she muttered. "Can you believe that? The nerve, telling me how to raise my own children."

Penelope didn't reply. The man had been upset, and had acted inappropriately, but something about the ready assault from Daphne was difficult to understand. What if he had kids at home? They were probably better-behaved than Peter. She watched him for a moment, sulkily putting shoes back into boxes and attempting to straighten the stack. Why wasn't Daphne helping?

"Earth to Penelope," Daphne said.

Penelope felt a touch on her shoulder, and turned to face the woman.

"You doing okay? Jake was saying that the church is looking for a new secretary. I could put in a word for you, if you like…"

"No, thank you. That's nice but I'm doing fine."

"You sure? It pays $50,000, and some of the single men at church are very good-looking!" Daphne winked.

How could this woman be so cruel one moment and do someone a favor the next? Penelope shrugged.

"I'm not ready for a full-time schedule. I do spend a lot of time on my art," she explained.

"Well, if you change your mind it may last another few weeks. You know they'll only hire someone with a good reference from a member." Shrugging, she added, "I know a few men you might be interested in. I don't see a ring on that finger!"

Penelope smiled at her friend's charm.

"I'm actually dating someone I like," she lied.

"You know, I met Jake at church. I had just moved out here, and I didn't know anybody. He offered to show me around town a bit, and before you know it he had proposed! His family has a lot of money, and he's a lawyer so he doesn't do badly himself," she nudged Penelope in the ribs with her elbow, grinning enormously.

"That's great," Penelope said. It was all she had left. Daphne rambled off another few minutes' worth of small talk, and then Peter was tugging on her arm asking for the bathroom. As they waved goodbye to each other, Penelope's stomach turned over.

Standing, she began the long walk home. She'd come here in such pleasant spirits! *I know, deep down, that I'm not any different from that man who she cut down earlier. I wonder how long it will take him to recover? I wonder if he knows she just as easily said all the same things to me.*

Penelope pushed the main door open, looking out into an overcast sky. *I know I'm the kind of trash that could end up on the street somewhere. I don't want to go up where Daphne did. I don't want to climb that filthy capitalist ladder.*

She trudged onward, toward her home. The sun began to peek through the clouds a bit, and the sight was enough to make her smile. *I know that misery is not enough to break me. I suppose I live this way because I want to be truly miserable. That way, I can spit upon misery and laugh at my broken self. In the end, it's just another thing to experience.*

Unlocking the front door of her small apartment, Penelope looked around. The easel next to the patio door, the unwashed wineglasses on the coffee table. The old, tattered sofa. The art on the wall – art she remembered painting! The apartment itself was the symbol she'd been looking for. *In the end, misery is just another chance to dominate my world. To turn filth and poverty into beauty and home. More than that, it teaches me about myself.*

She snapped the deadbolt into place, setting her bag on the coffee table as she crossed the room. Picking up the charcoal, she began to sketch the man gathering his shoeboxes on a canvas. *Tranquility,* she thought. Before the image could slip her mind, she switched to a clean canvas and made a quick sketch of the profile of Daphne's face.

"I'll call this one The Monster Wears Make-Up," she said to herself out loud.

PUNCHLINES

The rain fell upon the rooftops and dumpsters alike, beating upon cars, trees, alleys and restaurants. Down over the lawns of the wealthy and the yards of the poor it quietly cascaded, perfectly rhythmic, as if in a dream.

Michael Huffman was a graduate of Stanford University, class of '78. He had soared above other minds in his classes as he put together his Literature major but after school, he thought, something had gone horribly wrong. Now, more than thirty years later, Michael Huffman missed his wife and child.

"Dang kids," Michael swore under his breath.

His mustache was gray and partially offset by the three days' growth of beard he failed to notice even as he turned and stared into the mirror. The other man was surprisingly old and appeared to be very angry even when, as now, his face wore no particular expression; reminding Michael that he didn't care much to look in the mirror anymore.

He scooped the refuse out of the urinal with a gloved hand and deposited it in a trash can, peeling off the latex glove on his way to the sink. He washed his hands for a long time under hot water and quickly tied up the trash bag, throwing the paper towel and inside-out glove in first. He put it on top of a pile of others and pushed the gray plastic wheelbarrow outside to throw each bag, one by one, into the dumpster.

Michael stood under the awning next to the wheelbarrow, slightly damp from his work yet not ready to go inside. His work complete, he leaned against a wall and peered into the now-driving rain. He closed his eyes, looking the part of his frustration, and his thoughts raced to torment him about being a middle-aged failure who was forced to clean up other people's shit for a living. A moment later, a melody caught his ear and he opened his eyes, turning his head to hear it. Someone was singing in the rain outside the elementary school. The rain slowed, and Michael ventured out a distance from under the overhang to tell the kids to knock it off and go home, wherever they were.

As he began to hear the words more clearly, Michael realized he couldn't see the singers anywhere. Though their melody was sad, the song they sang was taunting, a childish song that made his blood boil. Feeling vaguely unsettled, Michael slowly wandered around the whole building in the light rain, looking above it and into the windows. He turned his gaze outward, but never caught a glimpse of whoever it was producing the music he heard; music that never got louder or quieter no matter where he walked.

"It's raining, it's pour-ring," the unseen children sang, over and over nearby, moving to lead him in one direction or another. "The old man is snoring. He went to bed so we shot him in the head and he wouldn't get up in the mor-ning."

Michael felt a chill at the conscious realization that someone was trying to lead him away from the school. Realizing next that he was soaked, the only logical choice was to walk back into the school to change and go home. The voices stopped as soon as he turned around.

Michael shuddered and tried to put the voices out of his mind. He put on fresh clothes from his locker; the pants and shirt he had worn to school that morning. Moments later he signed his name on a paper sheet confirming that the school was clean and left, carrying the uniform in one hand and an umbrella in the other. As he exited the building, he thought he heard the voices again. He turned around, and they stopped. Cautiously, he made his way home through the downpour.

That night, Michael couldn't sleep. He was reeling at the possibility of his mind being fallible. Perhaps he was going schizophrenic. He was a janitor at a public school and the stress of feeling that he needed to improve his station was driving him insane.

The stink of his failure to advance was simply too much to bear. Thoughts of the day just passed and the stark contrast his current life bore to the dreams of his youth some thirty years ago were just too prevalent, rearing their ugly heads time after time in his overheating mind.

In the end, he tossed and turned for two hours before he got up to sit on the porch. Observing the placid rain made him tired after a few minutes soon he was back in bed, tossing and turning as the winds picked up and the storm resumed its thunderous fury. Michael's thoughts accelerated as if they were racing.

Restless, he grew uncomfortable first in one position and then in another.

At last, a fitful state of rest was attained. Michael slept in motion, hands and feet beating against imaginary padded walls.

His eyes moved rapidly under their lids, attempting to penetrate the mystery he knew was a hoax. Children sang, and Michael followed. They sang and sang and soon he walked into a large steel cage, the door slamming shut behind him.

He wailed and cried and eventually drew the conclusion that he had been put into a mental institution to be treated for schizophrenia.

"I'm not schizophrenic," he moaned, asleep. In the dream, he sat down and leaned against the wall, daring to remember the dream in his failing understanding of the reality that he lived. Angry, frustrated, Michael stood in front of the door, staring out the small window in the padding. He couldn't see what was on the other side. Straining, his eyes failed him and the blackness sucked him into its yawning depth through the three-inch square hole.

Suddenly, lightning struck very near the house. Its thunder shattered the night, annihilating the dream and simultaneously spurring Michael into action by justifying his restlessness.

Having forgotten the dream, Michael found a reason to persist in wakefulness. He quickly got out his legal pad and a pencil. He walked as quickly as possible to his recliner on the porch, knowing that the trance would be his and it was time to write the thoughts that harassed him.

It has been a long time since last I sat down with the mere intention of setting my thoughts to the page. Misery has cost me greatly, I fear. For it is a choice to be miserable in this life, so rich and full of encounters. We each choose what to give and what to take from our experiences every day. I try in vain to steal the attention of the horde of familiar strangers that surround me. I look to the future in hopes, once again, of finding solace in the days to come. The night impenetrable to a ray of hope is black indeed. Yet no one avails. No one wants to hear my mad ramblings this time and I turn my attention to the page in hopes of purging these demons from my soul.

So many illusions to create and to perceive. So many witnesses avail themselves to call down a blatant wrongdoer – so many blind eyes they have for the suffering of one in their midst. I have worked to be at peace with the present by seeking to determine a path to the future, using the past as my guide. Such a course of action is taken in vain, however, and herein lies the source of my frustration.

Identified but not dispersed, the ghastly horrors in the night remain unwavering. They watched my young days, my reveling and my self-righteous struggle yet they did not present themselves until the party had died. I am a remarkable man. A remarkable farce has been my life. If, indeed, it is all a divine comedy, I fear my moments have been punchlines, making me the butt of the joke.

But never fear! At last I find myself ready for bed. Thank you, blank page, for allowing me that which my soul mates cannot give – an audience to the interminable suffering that goes, unbeknownst to the world, on and on in my thoughts.

Feeling better, Michael finished reading his new creation and walked back inside to the refrigerator to pour a glass of water. He set a glass on the counter and then paused for a minute, staring into the open refrigerator and leaning on the door. It was hard work, writing down feelings he had repressed for years. A former novelist, Michael had taken the job as a janitor in order to allow himself a little financial peace of mind as he worked toward his masterpiece. Then, one day, he'd just stopped. He'd gotten a woman pregnant and married her and had begun to raise a child. Then, they had left and Michael's world had stopped.

He poured a glass of water from the gallon jug he kept in the fridge. Grief could be a terrible thing. Now his mind was clear and he planned to write even more, later. He walked into the bedroom, sipping the water and enjoying the contented feeling he got from setting his thoughts to rest. Michael was asleep as soon as his head hit the pillow and in the morning, he awoke, feeling rested and refreshed as the sun beamed in through the window. The storm had ended and Michael set to his morning routine with a smile on his face.

He walked out the door a few minutes later, setting a battered briefcase down in the hallway to fish in his pocket for his keys. It contained a legal pad, two ballpoint pens, a copy of <u>Great Expectations</u>, and his lunch in addition to the umbrella. Michael slipped his keys into his pocket and picked up the briefcase before he walked into the sun, humming. Later, there was supposed to be more rain.

DISINTEREST

I was in the hospital long enough that my parents started going back to work. At first, I had been worried that I wouldn't get better – but here it was, the last day of my stay.

I'd been in for about a week, at that point, and the doctors were only keeping me there to observe me. I had a broken leg and a pulmonary embolism, both more or less directly caused by being run over. I guess that's why I started thinking so much. That and the doctors. Ever since I'd been little, my parents and teachers asked me to try extra hard so that I could become something special.

"You're smart, Kristen. Quit goofing off so much," Mrs. Thompson had said.

That was over ten years ago, now, I thought. What the hell happened to me? I was twenty-five, and working in a gas station. I drank to excess, dated idiots, and bounced from one job to the next.

The way the doctors moved, though, the way they treated me. Something about it seemed so... *genuine*. I could tell that their lives held a structure mine didn't. I was jealous, at first, but as I mentally berated myself for never listening back in school it occurred to me that I'd *never* felt that way. About anything. Having that, and losing it, sure. Maybe that's a good reason to feel jealous – but I didn't know thing one about what it was like to have a purpose.

I studied them, after that moment. I was awake at 5:00 in the morning because my nurse had come in to give me some pills. I was so excited to leave the hospital I probably couldn't have slept anyway. She was blonde and pretty, maybe even a few years younger than I was.

"Here's the medication to thin your blood. It's been several days, but if there are any more clots we can't be too careful," she said with a smile.

"Yes, ma'am," I'd replied without thinking.

Ma'am? The woman was clearly not old enough to be a *ma'am.* Maybe the way she looked at me, that mix of business and care, maybe that was what demanded such respect even from a miscreant like myself. The door to the room was open, and I could them walk by every so often. Such a quick step. Every single person on staff had things to do, and I hadn't seen anyone goof off or seem hung over the entire time I'd been here.

I was uneventfully discharged later that day. My mom gave me a ride back home, and after a bit of pampering, mercifully left me alone with my thoughts. I promptly fell asleep.

When I woke up, it was time for work. I'd missed a month and Brian would probably fire me if I didn't show up. I was the clerk at a convenience store – easily replaceable if I became inconvenient. I pulled out my phone and requested a ride from the local rideshare service.

After I'd gotten settled in at work, my thoughts started flowing again in earnest. There was a light rain falling, and it was doing a great job at keeping people from coming into the store. I pulled out my phone, ready to check up on social media or something, but nothing there held my interest. I found myself staring out the window, wondering what I could do to improve my life. It was no good coming back here to be locked up indoors for fifty hours a week.

The nurses were the ones who had really impressed me, I reflected. The doctors, sure, they made far more money – but the nurses were engaged, they *cared*! They also didn't need to go to school for so long. I pictured them in my head. The way they sped around, had my life been a graphic novel, could have been represented by bold capital letters:

BUSY! BUSY! BUSY!

It wasn't even just the nurses who impressed. Doctors, receptionists, janitors, technicians, therapists – even their customer service people seemed more engaged than the ones who worked elsewhere. And, come to think of it, policemen and EMTs and firefighters all seemed to display that same sort of engagement. Maybe that was why there were so many television shows about them.

So, even people who didn't do jobs like those were fixated on them. Was that because most work is so tedious and boring? Were the rest of us just jealous of the ones whose jobs are *worth* doing?

I couldn't imagine a doctor quitting work because he had made enough money. I couldn't imagine one – no matter how wealthy – giving up the importance of practicing whatever kind of medicine he was good at.

How it must feel to be so valuable!

And then, I thought, you have jobs like the ones I end up doing. It's no wonder I'm always bouncing from this one to the next – I'm looking for that sense of purpose and none of them give it to me.

Then another thought struck me.

I act out, too!

I pictured the incident in my head. My boyfriend, after drinking too much, had started driving before I'd gotten in the car. I'd started running, gotten the door open, tripped, and somehow put my right leg under the rear passenger side wheel.

Idiots.

What on earth were you thinking? What about him?

I might be a healthier, saner person if I had something important to do. Maybe Nick would too. I guess I get bored, and I act like an idiot to entertain myself. I ruminated on that thought for a minute, thinking of the times I'd almost gotten arrested for tagging, for vandalizing things that weren't mine. As I'd gotten older, it had turned mostly into seeing how drunk I could get. And, as it often turned out, that was pretty drunk.

It's fun, sometimes, though…

The thought wouldn't let go. It was true. I didn't hate my life, or myself, or really anyone at all.

WHAM!

I was disturbed from my reverie by the sound of the door slamming all the way open. I looked away from the window for a moment, too shocked to make a sound aside from the gasp that sucked itself out between my lips. A man in a ski mask stood across the counter from me, his hand in his coat pocket. He put a canvas bag on the counter, but I couldn't move yet.

"Hi. This is a robbery," he said.

"Erm. Haha. Uhhh," I was still fairly dumbstruck.

"Cash, please," he continued.

"Oh. Um. Right. Haha," I said, unable to stop the nervous giggle.

I left my broken leg propped up on the stool in its cast and leaned forward, reaching for the bag. The man stood there, watching me as I pressed the 'NO SALE' button on the register. There wasn't a lot of cash inside. I scooped out the twenties first, but when I got to the coins the man stopped me.

"Not the coins. Is there anything else I can get at?" His tone still wasn't terribly aggressive.

"Um. I guess you can grab a soda if you want?" I shrugged. "Or some cigarettes?"

"Hahaha that's great. Uh, yeah, grab me two cartons of those," he said, pointing.

"Ok," I replied.

The man turned and walked to the soda fountain. He poured himself a large soft drink. I decided that, as far as robbers went, this guy wasn't so bad. I put the cigarettes in the bag with the money, and handed it to him as he came back to the register. He mimed a tip of his hat to me, and went to leave the store.

"Have a nice day," he said.

"You too." I couldn't help but smile a little. And I swear, he looked back at me, winked at me, as he walked out the door.

THE CURSED FORTUNE

John Paul sat and ate the best Chinese food he had ever had. His old friend, Tommy Bolinger had invited him out to a fancy place and treated him to a quality meal. The two men had graduated high school a few years before and Tommy had gone off to college but John Paul had no desire to do this, yet. The meal had been fantastic, but John Paul needed to go to work.

"Well, buddy, it was sure very nice to see you."

John Paul agreed. "Yeah, thanks again for lunch. I hope things keep going your way, man. It's inspiring to see how well you're doing."

The waitress brought the check and a pair of fortune cookies, one of which was eagerly mauled by John Paul. He popped the cellophane wrapper and pulled the cookie apart. Tommy chuckled at his friend as he signed the receipt.

John Paul's face became a mask of confusion when Tommy looked up.

"It's bad luck to be superstitious," he read, laughing.

Tommy laughed too, recalling that John Paul had been analytic to the point of neurosis in high school.

"I'm sure you'll agree with that!" Tommy watched his friend's mirth carefully.

"Yeah," John Paul was saying. "I was pretty obsessed with that stuff, back in high school. I don't know how I was able to live like that."

"Well, since you like them so much, take mine too. I've never been very superstitious at all." Tommy handed John Paul his cookie, complete with cellophane wrapping, then stood.

John Paul followed, opening the second cookie and chuckling. He tossed the cookie and its wrapper into the trash can near the door as they walked outside, but as he began to read the slip of paper, his eyes opened wide with shock. He read the fortune out loud to Tommy:

"You will perish with the sun tonight, but YOU will not rise tomorrow."

Tommy chuckled. "That's what it says? Damn. Heavy. Good thing there's no way for those things to be accurate."

"Man, this is really freaking me out. Count the words – 13. Oh and look at the lucky numbers: 13, 49, 58, 67, 76, 85, 94, 139, 148, 157, 166, 175, 184 – there are 13 of them and they all add up to thirteen!" John Paul had always been very good at arithmetic. His low-level interest in numerology had its roots in a movie he had watched years ago. "This has to be some kind of curse!"

"Let's get out of here, forget about it. It's garbage." Tommy turned to walk to his car, unable and unwilling to allow John Paul to begin to vent these pointless anxieties again.

John Paul followed him, but with a slight reluctance. He held on to the fortune as they left the restaurant. As he waved goodbye to Tommy, John Paul noticed a tan Chevrolet pickup truck with a black grill guard and a license plate that said KLR-13S. He briefly shuddered, then drove himself home to get ready for work.

The day went by without anything interesting happening, but that same tan, mid 1990's Chevrolet with the black grille guard was sitting in this parking lot too. As a bagger, John Paul saw a lot of cars in the parking lot and nothing was amiss with him, yet. Then the shift was ending and he was doing the put-backs, taking things that people had opted out of purchasing in the checkout lines back out to the shelves. Things were going fine until he walked under a ladder.

"What the..."

John Paul had been walking along the aisle where the canned goods were kept, and the ladder – which had no evident purpose – spanned most of the aisle. It was over ten feet tall, and someone had just left it there.

John Paul's fragile, cautious mood immediately turned to anger. He gave up on the task of finding the places for all of the items and instead simply set two cans of green beans on the nearest shelf along with some bubble gum, toothpaste, a box of tampons. Then he went into the break room, clocked out, and left for the day. As he walked out to his car, he couldn't seem to help repeatedly looking back over his shoulder.

He locked the door behind him, securing each of three dead bolts and wedging the kick-bar under the doorknob. He had seen the truck again, in the parking lot of his apartment complex this time. John Paul laughed at himself. What was this anxiety caused by? Was it really because today was Friday the 13th? *It's bad luck to be superstitious*, he chided himself with a chuckle. Curses weren't a real thing. Then he went about his business, cleaning the small apartment and feeling no horror when it came time to walk past the truck on his way to the dumpster with the bag of trash. He was still laughing to himself about the truck when he stuck his hand into the bright yellow box to pull out a white trash bag. Only, this was the last bag in the box. He opened it, installed it into his white trash can and went to put the box inside.

It rattled.

John Paul looked inside, reached his hand in to see what was causing the rattle. He pulled out a small, roundish thing and a crumpled piece of paper. The roundish, smooth object was a doll of some sort, dressed in pink with a bright yellow face. The paper, now un-wadded, had some words on it but they looked like maybe Chinese? He couldn't read them. As he moved to throw the document away, icy needles poked his neck. He stopped cold, in a fit of superstitious anxiety. Surely one of the roommates had simply left it there, but who could it have been?

Examining the note further, John Paul's nerves got the better of him. He walked into the hall, and down a few doors to a neighbor's apartment. The knocks sounded hollow and far too loud in the unusually quiet early evening. Mr. Yin was a Chinese immigrant with white hair and a talent for computer languages, who had paid John Paul to help him move in earlier that year. The two had a distant friendship, as a result of John's efforts to learn to code. As the older man opened the door, he inclined his head and ushered in the lanky twenty-five-year old.

"Good to see you, John Paul. Come in, sit down," he said, gesturing to an overstuffed chair.

"Thanks. You too, Mr. Yin. How's your wife?"

"She's good. What brings you over this evening?"

John Paul held out the wrinkled piece of paper. "It's a long shot, but I've had an odd day. Do you know what this says?"

"Oh, it is Mandarin!" Mr. Yin was excited. He picked up a pen and a notepad, leaning over the coffee table, and began to write on a piece of paper. "Ni, hen, meh," he muttered. He took his time translating the note and made puzzled faces. "I do not understand, but I've written out some translations," he said, finishing.

"What do you mean, Mr. Yin?"

"Very strange indeed. Could be a fortune cookie fortune?" Mr. Yin exclaimed, in his foreign accent. "Where did you get this paper?"

"It was in my garbage bag box, w-with this," John Paul fumbled, pulling the figurine out of his pocket.

"Weird," said Mr. Yin, a puzzled look on his face.

John Paul shrugged. "Do you want to see the little doll that was in there with it? I got a fortune earlier that said I would die, basically," he elaborated with a chuckle, hoping to find some sympathy.

Mr. Yin stood up, refusing to examine the figurine. He paced for a moment, hands on his hips. "You have to go now. Mrs. Yin is almost home. It's almost seven o'clock." He pointed at the clock. "We have dinner plans. Come back later and we can talk more."

As the door slammed behind John Paul, he thought he heard the old man laughing quite hysterically on the other side. The translation was not helpful. It was covered in phrases like "You are very beautiful," and "Ill luck follows you today." Others suggested committed relationships and said that fortune smiled in his direction, but John Paul's thoughts remained fixed upon that second one even as he read the others.

Back in his apartment, John Paul sat in his recliner, studying the small figurine. It was a strange statuette of an Asian girl, almost perfectly round, with distinctly slanted eyes and long black braids. She was laughing at him. John Paul did not know what to make of her. He wondered where she had come from. Suddenly, he realized she made him distinctly uneasy. He set her on the coffee table.

He got up and went into the kitchen. He opened the fridge, poured himself a glass of juice, and looked at the clock on the microwave. 7:13, it said. Today was Friday, July 13th. The combination of lucky and unlucky numbers made John Paul uneasy at the best of times but now it added substantially to his growing sense of horror. Why was the old numerology gag so inescapable today?

He felt the doll staring at him from the coffee table but when he looked back she was gone. Where was she? He turned, scanning the room, and his head impacted a still-open cupboard door. He grabbed his head with both hands in shock, then realized he had dropped the glass of lemonade to shatter on the floor. *Relax*, he soothed himself. Maybe he should go out for a cigarette. He'd clean up the mess in a moment.

He sat on the balcony of his seventh story apartment looking out over the roads and the city, a cigarette in between the first two fingers of his trembling right hand. The day had been full of odd coincidences, but his mind couldn't stop wondering where the doll was. Perhaps some days nothing was going to make sense – but perhaps there was something at work here. He couldn't shake the feeling.

"Jesus, John Paul. You need to get a handle on it," he muttered to himself.

There he was, wasting his Friday night on pointless anxiety. He didn't have to work tomorrow. Why hadn't he even thought about going out tonight? Flicking the half-smoked cigarette over the railing of the balcony, John Paul resolved to go to the bar across the street. He could simply walk over there and the place would be full of his friends and neighbors. That would ease his nerves until it wasn't Friday the 13th anymore and then he could get it together.

Back inside the apartment, John Paul took a towel and used it to mop up the juice on the floor. He made a fried egg sandwich, and ate it as quickly as he could. Then he took a can of beer from the fridge to drink in the shower. Despite taking his time in the shower, John Paul had dressed and made it out the door at 8:01.

The elevator was slow, which was why John Paul was looking at his watch, seeing yet another strange coincidence and wondering at his bad luck that it should be 8:05 now.

Moments later, the tan Chevrolet pickup with the black grille guard sat, idling, in the middle of the street. The man wondered how the cell phone could have rung at that particular moment, diverting his eyes from the road just long enough for this boy to

111

make his fatal mistake. Rising from the driver's seat, somnambulant, he made his was to John Paul's side.

He got there right before the last rays of the setting sun failed completely. The door ajar bell kept ringing, time after time, as the driver knelt over the boy who had stepped in front of his vehicle. He said nothing, shocked into silence. He studied the boy's face, unable to process the last few moments. He sat that way for a few moments, rocking and cradling John Paul Martin's dying head as he listened to the boy's last, whispered words.

"It's bad luck to be superstitious."

DRINKS ON THE HOUSE AT THE WINCHESTER

I sat in the bath, fully too tall to lie down unless I bent my knees all the way and even then it was too cozy. As the warm water heated my skin and I moved around, freshly exposed parts of me gave off light clouds of steam. I was relaxing, until I got the phone call. A few of my friends wanted to go out drinking and were under the impression I'd like to go along. That's all it was. No intention of murder, thievery or malice of any kind. Nights when you don't have such ill intentions are always the most fun; the ones where you do want to break the laws of boredom that ensnare the work-a-day world always end up being little or no fun. Guess it's all the planning you put into your big night out raising the expectations or something like that.

But anyway, as I was saying, it was just another night I'd have preferred to spend relaxing on my own terms and not caring. And now I was lazily getting into the backseat of a brand-new Kia. On the way to the first bar, nobody said much. It was like one of those boring road trips you take with a girlfriend's family, the first time you're really around them. Or the first forty times if you don't get along well with them. The people in the car were Jimmy, Danny and Kara. Jimmy Hawkins was a short little white guy with a shaved head and an athletic, aggressive bent to him; he would get sloppy drunk and drive us home without thinking twice and probably fight any cops that had something to say about it. He was sleeping with the beautiful, medium height brunette Kara Johnson, who already had one child and probably wouldn't mind hooking up with me or Danny at the moment. Danny Vasquez was the bass guitarist in a little band that played the bars in town without a singer and made a little bit of money anyway because they could get the reggae groove going and keep it up for hours on end. Danny was probably the most normal one of us, good-looks owing to his dark complexion, dark hair, and ready smile. He was probably 6 feet tall but of a slender build.

Jimmy would pick fights at the bars sometimes, expecting me and Danny to step in and clean it up for him. I gotta hand it to the guy, he was great at getting into trouble. Unfortunately for him, about three months ago I got a phone call and went to see my now-ex girlfriend just as he was starting in about a huge black guy's mother. I probably would have let him sort it out on his own even if I'd been there – I was actually a little surprised he wasn't harder on Jimmy. Anyway, he called Danny from jail after he got beat up and we both went down to bail him out, but he was still so mad at me he tried to kick my ass when we got him to his house.

When we got to the first bar, a place called Hemingway's, there was what I like to call a funk in the air. Nobody said much, Jimmy bought a round of drinks, and we sort of stood and made very small talk together.

I asked Danny, "So are the two of them an item?"

"I don't think so, Dick, you interested in her?" came the reply.

"Nah man I don't poach. I punch." I punched him on the arm, about 40%. He rocked to the side a little under the blow and grabbed the afflicted spot with his other hand, making an exaggerated face.

"Ow. Guess that's why they named you Dick, huh, ya fuckin dick?"

I laughed, and Danny turned around and went to the bar. I looked at Jimmy and Kara, but they were gone. Danny brought me another beer, but I just stood there for another fifteen minutes without saying anything to anyone. Some Friday night, I thought, just sipping my drink and doing nothing with myself. When I finished that drink, I went to the bar. The bartender working looked exceptional in her low-cut spaghetti strap shirt but the whole bar was full of guys staring at her and I suppose that's why she looked so angry.

"Nuther one, por favor," I pointed at my empty bottle and smiled at her. Nothin' but a beer. I turned around and walked toward the back of the crowd, lit a cigarette. I leaned against the wall and let the bass give me a back massage.

Jimmy came back into the bar, perhaps thirty minutes since I'd last seen him. He made sure I had a shot in one hand and a beer in the other, then turned to face me looking about as serious as I'd ever seen him.

"Yo, man, you got my back tonight? I may need you."

"Yeah whatever. I just want something to happen. Anything." I was noncommittal but generally, fights don't actually happen. When they do, I'm a head taller than the other drunk and that helps.

"Where'd Danny go?" Jimmy leaned up against the wall, draining his beer.

I shrugged and Jimmy took off. This bar sucks, I thought, looking around the room for any sort of female attention. The hip-hop soundtrack changed to disco. I took the shot, chugged the beer, and made another pass at Jessica, the bartender. I ordered a Jagerbomb and a beer. Ah, progress. She didn't charge me for the bomb. I smiled and tipped her big, then excused myself. My friends were M.I.A. but I had to piss so I shoved off from the bar and wandered toward the back of the overcrowded room.

Jimmy had gotten himself into trouble before, gambling mostly, but a few other things involving people wanting to hurt him had transpired over the years. For the most part he took care of himself, but tonight he was going to need help. He walked through the bar, having taken Kara home after she threw her drink in his face outside the Ladies' room earlier. He didn't know what she'd gotten so angry about but he had noticed the Lincoln Towncar that had followed him back up to the bar after he dropped her off. And the pair of jailbirds who had gotten out of it and headed toward the bar after him. He spied Danny flirting with a girl. The front door of the bar swung open. He chanced a glance – yep. The guys came in, both with shaved heads and dark clothes. He watched – nope. They walked around the crowd, away from the bar, looking for something. He grabbed Danny and pulled him the other direction.

"What the FUCK, man?" Danny fumed.

"Shut the fuck up man! I think Kara's ex-husband is here. She was pissed for no reason earlier so I had to take her home."

"Who the fuck is Kara's ex-husband?"

"Real bad news. Name is Rock Taylor. He was locked up for a while and started hanging out with those Nazi fucks, but he stayed wrapped up in it after he got out. Let's go find the Dick, maybe he can protect us." Danny shut up and followed Jimmy back to the bar, looking for Dick.

I took a nice, long piss. The first one of the night. I broke the seal, and consequently would have to piss more often in the coming hours. A couple of rough looking guys shouldered past me as I made my way back up to the bar, looking for Jimmy and Danny. I spotted them near the front door and stumbled in their direction.

"Where've you assholes been? Where's Kara?" I slurred.

"Tell you later. Let's go, next bar."

"This place sucks anyway." I threw my empty beer bottle at a trash can, missed it by a few feet, hit a guy in the stomach. He doubled over in shock, but nobody cared. I just laughed and walked out the door after my friends.

"Are they coming?" Jimmy slammed his door and started the car. I had just sat down in the back seat but I was starting to wake up because my friends were so excited. Jimmy threw the car into reverse and slammed the gas to the floor, peeling out of the parking spot. Danny was looking out the back window past me and just as I turned to see what he was looking at he started yelling "Go-go-go-go-go-go, NOW, JIMMY!!"

I saw several people walking out of the bar, nobody I knew, and, shrugging I turned back to face the front seat.

"So, now that we know who's following us, where should we go?" Jimmy was worried. I could practically feel the tremors in his voice.

I decided right then and there that something was going on, but they weren't letting me in on just what it was. I looked out the back window again, nothing but headlights to see. I mentally shrugged and turned back around.

"Dude, there's no way. Those guys beat people up for a living. Either one of them could take the three of us one handed!" Jimmy was nearing hysterics.

Then Danny spoke up. "When zombies attack, where else could we go but the Winchester?"

"What the fuck is the Winchester?" Jimmy hadn't been going out with us lately. Spending a lot of time with the extremely lovely Kara. I closed my eyes and pictured her – beautiful. She didn't feel the same way Jimmy did, but he was too charming to really put her off. So, she'd bide her time and do what every girl Jimmy started on with his charms eventually did – find someone else. Fucking Jimmy, always getting into fights, always trying to get every girl in the room. That guy's got a problem. He's too short.

By the time my thoughts caught up to my friends, we were getting out of the car in front of Balls to the Walls – my favorite pool hall in the area and temporarily the honorary Winchester. I usually knew most of the patrons there, and Danny knew a few of the guys. We called it the Winchester because we went there when we were bored with our lives – the joke being that zombies were attacking that day.

"Yeah man, the Winchester. If we're going to get mugged and beat up, we might as well do it on our turf!" I blurted.

I was jubilant.

My friends just glared at me and stomped off into the bar.

Inside the Winchester, there is a wall full of liquor behind a bar with plenty of ashtrays. There are enough big sticks to equip a Roman Centurion and fourteen or fifteen pool tables. Jimmy and Danny sit at the deserted bar and order a few drinks. I go to the restroom after the first beer to take a piss, once again, probably half an hour after the last time. That, as usual, means I've been drinking too hard tonight. I piss for what seems like an hour and it feels great. Then, I leave the restroom and play a dollar in the juke box. Three great songs for a dollar. Nothing like it in the world, especially when, since the bar is pretty much empty tonight without the usual pool club meeting, my songs come up first.

I walk around the corner of the bar as my first song comes on, Mick already wailing on the vocals to "Get Off My Cloud."

These two bruiser guys are standing face to face with my two friends, yelling at them. I'm already ballistic, and as I stride purposefully toward them, the guy on the left gives Danny a shove. My world turns red. I fly through the room, screaming at the top of my lungs.

"I don't give a FUCK who the FUCK you think you ARE," I bellow, staggering forward with astonishing grace and impressive speed – especially if you take into consideration my utter lack of sobriety.

The guy who dealt the shove to Danny gets a good old wiry guy punch to the nose from my friend in return for the shove, and when his eyes open back up he sees me flying toward him out of nowhere.

"But if ANYBODY is going to push this mother FUCKER around, it'll be ME, GODDAMN IT."

With that, I give the guy a shove. He's either still shocked that Danny had the balls to pop him one, or maybe my sudden screaming entrance to music surprised him. I shove him into his friend, somehow managing to capitalize completely on their surprise.

Badass #2 has now become entangled in Badass #1 and they both seem to trip over each other on the floor. That's how I know they've been drinking heavily, generally a no-no if you want to actually be able to fight. I give #2 a kick in the ribs, but #1 comes up quick. I'm somehow ready, so he launches himself at me – straight into a headlock. I let his momentum carry him past as I pivot, still hanging onto my headlock. I allow my body to be pushed toward the bar. With a crack like a sledgehammer splitting concrete, his head hits the bar. He hits the ground and stays there.

By this time, I'm laughing. Everyone else, about six people, is staring at me as I stand, rather calmly, in front of the hooligan with the bloody nose. I'm still laughing my head off.

He gives me a final glance and makes a quick decision to spend the next few minutes trying to drag his concussed friend out of the bar. We all just stand there and watch. My friends are silent, but still I laugh. Then they're gone, and things get quiet.

Danny breaks the silence. "Hey, Shannon, I think he needs a drink."

"Shit, Dick. That wasn't even much of a fight. I liked it! This one's on the house. What'll it be, champ?" She's smiling at me in a way I haven't been smiled at in far too long.

"Well, if it's on the house... better make it three shots of Patron!" This earns me a few high fives from my friends who are still nervously laughing. I'm in a great mood. People are still looking at me, but I can understand that. I'm not even wondering if those creeps are going to come back with a gun, or what they want, or why they decided to mess with us in the first place.

Shannon serves me three shots of strong tequila and, as I start to hand one to Danny, she interrupts, "Hey, those drinks are for YOU! Danny's already got his."

I lift the first tequila to my lips, lick the salt, take the shot and bite the lime. Shot glass down on the bar. Second tequila, same way as the first. Shit. I look around the bar, but Shannon and the guys are all watching so I down the third shot without lime or salt or anything. A girl and two guys get up and leave, like there's any reason to think crazy shit's about to go down. I yell something insulting at those pansy bastards as they walk out an hour before closing. Shannon laughs and smiles at me and I smile back, getting lost in those brown eyes. I guess all the pretty girls are bartenders because it pays so well.

"Say, Dick, you hear me?"

I realize my eyes are closed. They pop open a second later and Shannon hands me a Jell-O shot. The only people left in the bar are me and her. It's closed, I realize. She pulls a pipe out from behind the bar and loads a bowl of strong weed, hands it off to me. I smile and take a rip, then pass it back. Shannon hits the pipe, gets us each another Jell-O shot, and walks around to stand right in front of me.

"I like you, Dick." She is smiling at me, and she looks like a cross between an angel from heaven and one from Victoria's Secret. But I'm trying to figure out how this all got started. She hands me a Jell-O shot and down the hatch it goes, then a rip off the ole pipe and then a cigarette and suddenly Shannon's finger lands on my chin and I realize I've been staring at the ceiling for at least a minute, slowly spinning in a partial circle.

She pulls my face close to hers just as her last comment finally registers in my slowed-down mind. I open my mouth to assert that she likes Dick – a favorite joke of mine after a few too many – but no words come out. Just puke. Green puke. Lots and lots of green puke. It gets in Shannon's mouth. It runs down Shannon's shirt, leaking into her ample cleavage. I'm screaming as I turn my head midstream, and more puke shoots over the bottles to hit the mirror behind the bar. It stinks.

The next morning, I woke up at Shannon's apartment, on the couch, a towel underneath me to save it from the puke that covers the front of my shirt. I don't know how I got there, but I'm fairly certain she didn't decide to sleep with me after all. As I pulled the nasty shirt off and used it to wipe my face, Shannon walked in through the front door.

"Hey, Dick! Good morning, ya fuckin' dick!"

"Ughhh.... Headache..."

Shannon smiled at me, laughing. "I know a cure for that!"

Brightened by her mood, I stood up. She opened the front door and motioned for me to leave. I checked my pockets. Phone, gone. Keys, gone. Wallet, empty, but still technically accounted for. That's actually an improvement for the three of us – one weekend we lost my car. I started walking and Shannon slammed the door behind me, locking the deadbolt. As I made it to the street, the bright early sun hit my retinas, causing so much pain I wondered for a second if I had been bitten by a vampire last night. I passed Danny's house on my way home but nobody was there. Then I got to Jimmy's, a little out of the way, but I wanted to sit down and it was closer than my place.

After a slow, painful eternity I arrived at the front door, missing shirt, completely hung over and looking like shit to boot. Kara answered my knock.

"Oh, hey, if it isn't that fucking DICK that broke my ex-husband's skull last night!" she shrieked at me, causing a definite flinch on my part. When I open my eyes, the door is wide open and all three of my best friends are laughing. They invited me in, I ate

123

scrambled eggs with them, and then Kara volunteered to take me home after the meal. I got in her car and we started driving. With absolutely no warning, I threw up what looked like pieces of old, dried sponge (partially digested eggs) in a thick coat of bile (used to be liquor) that smelled like a mixture of diarrhea and kerosene (I still don't know why it smelled so *bad*) onto the windshield, onto the dashboard, onto the airbag.

To her credit, Kara didn't scream. She stared. The way a deer stares at the car that's about to run it down. But she didn't stare long; instead of that, she hit a parked car and the airbag went off.

To the best of my knowledge, everything in this story is the whole, legitimate truth. As best as I can gather, it is, anyway. Parts are my own memory; the rest was told to me by my friends over the next few days when they visited me in the hospital. I knew it was a bad deal when there were drinks on the house at the Winchester.

That scrambled egg vomit was thrown through my left eye by the airbag. Pretty serious injury, really. They said I was lucky to be alive, and that I might wind up with frontal lobe damage as a result. I ended up losing the eye. So, now my depth perception is ruined and there are at least two more beautiful women in this world who will never, under any circumstances at all, ever, EVER sleep with me – but I figure what the hell, at least I got a story out of the deal.

I'm clean and sober now, have been for a lot of years at this point. Whenever anyone gives me a hard time about not drinking, I just laugh a little bit and walk away.

OBLIVION

Devon Wallace was an imaginative youth of fourteen years. Sometimes his thoughts ran wild, just like anybody else's. They would circle themselves and spin away into a nonsensical oblivion if he followed them for long enough. He had been picked on at school today, and felt the world could end any moment.

Martin Harrison was in love with Erika Wallace, who danced at a high end local strip club. He certainly earned the thousand dollars he paid for their private session each week, but Erika didn't feel comfortable dating a customer—and Martin himself was quite ugly. Forty-three years old, he made his living by hacking computers. She thought he was fat and could scarcely stand his laugh.

His leather jacket slick with rain, he smashed a window in the back of the house where Devon and Erika lived. He took the iron and cleared out the shards of glass that poked up from the frame, then threw the tire iron into the room and hoisted himself over the threshold.

Devon heard the crash. Scrambling, he made the rapid decision that the noise had come from his own room. He was tall and lanky, though, and not coordinated enough to move quietly. As he dashed toward his bedroom door in the darkness of the silent house, his foot met with the puddle that always formed in the hall when it rained and slipped out from under him. Headlong, his head and arms made contact with a wall as he tried to brace himself. "Fuck!" he yelled, unable to help himself.

Martin heard the young man's scream, heard the crash that followed. He opened the door with his left hand, the tire iron still in his right. His iPhone had been pulled a little way out of one of his front pockets, and the flash was turned on to provide a bit of light.

Devon scrambled to his feet, assuming a defensive posture. He couldn't catch a glimpse of Martin's face because the LED on the back of the phone kept blinding him. He put a hand up, trying to cover the thing so that he could see his attacker's face.

"Who-who are you?" he gasped, his voice dripping with frustration and terror.

Martin burst out laughing. In all the hacking it had taken him to find Erika's address, and her phone number, he had never discovered she had a child. This made things so much easier!

"I'm Martin," he got in. His guffaws slowed, and he managed to force a serious tone into his voice. "I'm a friend of your mother's from work. Long story short, something very bad is happening tonight and we don't have time to discuss it. She'll be home any moment and when she gets here we're all going to get into my Maserati and drive for the mountains as fast as we can."

Martin dropped the tire iron and lit a candle he had in his pocket. He held his hands up so that Devon would understand that he meant no harm. A quick glance around the room revealed an open beer and a bag of chips at the computer desk. He wondered for a moment what game Devon had been playing.

"You aren't a friend," the youth began. "Friends don't cut the power to a house and then break in!"

"Shut the fuck up, kid. I am your friend – and I'm here to save her, as well as you! Have a seat, she'll be here any minute to explain all this to you." Martin sighed and stretched a bit, pacing. Erika was supposed to have been here by now. Where on earth was she?

Devon did as instructed, leaning back onto the leather couch. As Martin paced, the light from his iPhone shone on the tire iron on the floor for a moment.

"What are you supposed to be saving us *from*, again?"

Martin turned back to Devon, still pacing.

"Look. It sounds crazy, and we don't have time for that. Where's your mom?"

Devon sighed. Perhaps a sympathy play was in order? He let loose his emotions, tears running down his face.

"I just found out where she works," he mumbled through the tears. "She's been doing... that... all night!"

Martin placed a hand on Devon's shoulder, feeling the trembles of the young man's breath with each sob.

"Aw, shit. Well, kid, if it's any consolation for you, I went by the club earlier. She isn't working tonight."

Devon looked up, able to detect a serious expression on the man's face. He rubbed his eyes.

"Did she at least tell you when she was planning to be home?" Martin asked.

"Would you mind turning off that iPhone? Or maybe shining it somewhere other than my face?"

"Oh. Of course." Martin laid the phone face down on the coffee table, and for the first time Devon got a good look at him. It was absurd that he had been afraid of this short, pudgy, messy guy!

"Devon, where is she? I spoke with her before the lines went down and she said she would be here." Martin's voice was serious.

"No. I have no idea." Devon looked down. Suddenly, he looked back up – staring into Martin's eyes. "You look like a librarian. What did you say you were saving us from, again?"

Martin's stomach turned. He thought about his response for a moment, noting that Devon was both taller and more muscular that he was, although probably not even in high school yet. *I guess the kid's an athlete*, he thought, as anxiety overtook him.

"It's big! And they know! I'm not sure what's coming, not exactly, but their resources are leaving this area. I say me, you, and your mom go with them. I have a fast car. Maybe we'll even make it to my family's place, in Colorado. We'll be safe there until we figure out what's happening!"

Devon stared at him. Martin fell silent. Finally, the youth nodded and stood up.

"You're crazy. I guess you must have bought a dance from mom and somehow tracked her down, but you don't know her. And we're not going to Colorado with you." Devon began to pace. "Have a seat, Martin," he said. As the man took a step toward the recliner, Devon quietly bent down and recovered his tire iron. Just as Martin took his seat, Devon spun around. "I changed my mind. Get the fuck out of here. Go drive yourself to Colorado. I don't want you here when mom gets home."

Martin stood up and stared at his feet as he slowly walked to the front door. He picked his iPhone up from the coffee table and switched off its flashlight. There was no telling when Erika would be home, and things had gone from bad to worse. He would wait outside until she got home, then have her help him explain everything to Devon. He reached into his pocket, removing the keys to his Maserati.

Devon swung the tire iron just as Martin's hand latched onto the doorknob. The iron caught the older man at the base of the neck with a sick, heavy *whunk*. Martin slumped to the ground, his head inclined too far to the left.

Just then, a key entered the deadbolt. It unlocked the door, but the man's body was still in the way. Dumbstruck, Devon grabbed Martin's feet and dragged him aside.

Erika burst into the house, her cellphone flashlight illuminating the scene, and she let out a gasp when she saw what had happened.

"Devon?! What did you do? Noooo.... Not Martin!" she sobbed.

Devon hugged his mother, mumbling apologies. Suddenly, a bright blue light shone in through the open front door. His eyes widened as he continued to pat his mother on the back. There was a *hum*, an eerie pulse, and the blue light grew brighter.

"Mom, look!" Devon pointed.

Erika led the way into the front yard, and the two joined their silent neighbors in casting eyes skyward – then everything went dark again.

Across town, Dr. Edwin Mathis was leaving his office when he noticed the bright blue light. It was 11:45 PM, and the streets were deserted and silent. A piece of newspaper blew past in a sudden gust of wind, but Mathis stood there frozen and staring up into the sky. The moon was a bright shade of neon blue – then it began to pulse, slowly at first and speeding up, until it simply blinked out of sight and was gone.

Edwin's terror knew no bounds – it held him utterly frozen.

Without the moon's light, the night was suddenly still, and supernaturally dark.

All around the world, airlines failed to arrive at their destinations. Or, rather, they arrived at the coordinates to find that there was no landmass there anymore. All they could do was continue flying until the fuel ran out. Ocean liners that were still afloat lost all communications, doomed to drift aimlessly until the food ran out. A lone astronaut awakened on the space station. The first thing he noticed was that the Earth was entirely blue. Scratching his head, he went for coffee.

Somewhere, deep in space, the aliens who stole the moon were still laughing.

STILL

T he car idles in the parking lot. He stands, a few feet away, watching and smoking. She puts the car in reverse, pulls out of the space, and shifts it into drive. He watches as the car drives away. Then, he goes back into the apartment and begins to paint. His anger colors the work, giving it meaning.

She drives to a city far away. When she reaches the house a few hours after leaving the apartment, her father is outside waiting for her. This unusual occurrence punctuates the gravity of what has just transpired – the choice she made to end the post collegiate doldrums and resume the life she left. Independence from her parents is the goal; but to realize it, she must depend completely upon them for a time.

It is January in Texas. As she makes the long drive, Sarah notices the lack of flowers on the side of the road. The dormant vegetation suits her for the moment of reflection upon the previous eight months. It all started with a brain tumor diagnosed one year ago.

"That's awful," he said as he embraced her. She loved the smell of the cologne he wore. As she surrendered herself to his warm, strong body, she began to cry. The mother she had been fighting for five years for

133

her independence had been diagnosed with a remarkable lump of dead material between the hemispheres of her brain. An operation would take place in a few months, but the outlook was grim. Without the absolute best medical care there would be no chance for survival, and even with it, the likelihood of a full recovery was minimal.

They collapsed together, onto the bed her father had purchased for her when she graduated from college dormitories to apartment living.

"Are you OK?" he had asked. She wasn't annoyed with the question, but she did not respond immediately. He waited patiently.

"Yeah. I think so. I'm going to have to move back there."

"That's alright. I can come with." He smiled, tickling her. She felt awful, but it coaxed laughter out of the darkness of her soul.

Months later, the operation had been a stunning success. While recovery was not immediate, Sarah's mother did recover fully after a few weeks of physical therapy. The doctors hailed it as a miracle. The night before the operation, the couple had met Sarah's stepfather for dinner. It was the first time Bradley had ever tried sushi, and to his surprise, it was delicious. Sarah was delighted that he liked it. Although sake was not a new favorite beverage, wassabi proved an excellent remedy for the allergy-clogged sinus cavity that had plagued him since they arrived.

After dinner, the hospital awaited. It was immense. The two men doddered around smoking cigarettes and looking at the structure, the cars that passed by in front of it, the other people going rapidly to wherever they had to go to. Sarah watched them from a few paces behind her step-father and boyfriend. The very concept of the hospital was daunting in itself; not to mention the enormity of the situation at hand. She needed her mother to survive so that the two of them could make things right. It had been growing in her mind the past few years - a healthy relationship with her mother would be very good for each of them. Edward was worried about his new wife and longtime lover, and Bradley was as concerned for each of them as he was about the woman upstairs.

Finally, the trio went inside. Edward took the elevator, but Bradley accompanied Sarah up the stairs. There was a statue of the Christ blessing a woman done in bronze in the lobby, but as they walked past it the artist's sense of humor came to light. Sarah laughed and pointed the scene out to Bradley, the hand in line with the head in line with the holy crotch. He chuckled, photographing the statue from the appropriate angle with his phone, and led the way to the room where Edward awaited them.

A coffeepot sat on a counter inside the room. Edward had found coffee and water, but had difficulty making it work. Bradley eventually discovered that it was fed from a pipe in the wall, which explained why there was nowhere to put the water in.

"Here," said Edward, flipping a switch.

Nothing happened. He and Bradley exchanged a glance of defeat, and sat down near Sarah. Magazines and conversation dragged by, as the worried trio waited for visiting hours to begin. Finally, the appointed hour was at hand.

She was lying in a hospital bed just past the double doors behind a white curtain. The entire scene positively reeked of sterility, from the plastic paneling on the walls to the shiny, waxed linoleum flooring. A small TV was mounted to the wall, and there was only one chair. The woman on the bed looked deathly ill, covered up to her armpits in lightly colored hospital blankets. She had a white gown on and her skin looked very pale, but her blonde hair seemed true to Bradley's memory, anyway. Edward broke the ice.

"Sweetheart, you look terribly ill. Maybe we should cancel your breast implants." Elizabeth exploded into guffaws, breaking the silence she had maintained from the slow entrance of her entourage. Bradley and Sarah smiled, keeping their distance.

"I wonder if they'll let me keep the tumor. It might be an interesting conversation piece at the tennis court." Elizabeth was speaking slowly, but once her audience grasped the attempt at humor they began to chuckle with her.

At one point a nurse came by and checked on Elizabeth. Then, a seemingly short time later, she was back to remind the guests that visiting hours had ended and that they needed to leave.

Edward knelt by the bed, taking his wife's hand in his own. He professed his undying love for her in utter sincerity, and then stood to wish her a good night's rest. "You sure you don't want to trade

136

places?" By this point Edward had the other three laughing so hard that tears were brimming up around their eyes and, reluctantly, he followed them out of the hospital.

The trio got into Elizabeth's SUV and, driving, Edward began to regale the young couple with stories from his job as the district attorney's publicist.

"You know; we have this corpse down in the morgue named Stumpy. It's just a torso, male, with no arms or legs or head. But there is one identifying characteristic, a birth mark under the scrotum. Well, we advertised and advertised, but the thing was down there for ten years before we got anyone to come in to identify it. A woman walked in, asked to see the corpse, and walked straight to it as though she knew exactly who it was. The coroner pulled the sheet off the body, and she went straight to lifting up the scrotum and examined the marking there. She looked at the coroner, said 'Not him,' and walked straight out the door. We still don't know whose body that is!"

Bradley sobbed with laughter, and Sarah smiled. The next few days provided dramatically less mirth, but the operation went stunningly and the three of them were surrounded by other family and friends when the news was announced that everything was going to be fine. Somehow, against every chance, Elizabeth was well on her way to a full recovery.

Sarah had gotten certified to teach public school during the spring, under the impression that teachers were in demand. She wanted to be able to pick up to move closer to home, but her current job was not something she could transfer. Bradley worked as a delivery driver for an industrial company, which reminded him of prison. July came, and he quit the job. Besides a deep hatred for his boss, he had money saved and needed time to look for other work if they were to move. Sarah had hopes of multiple interviews in her home town, but July came and went with no word and so did August. She took a job teaching preschool. The couple moved into a new apartment together. Bradley started a business, which promptly imploded and left him destitute. Sarah grew sullen and moody, even as Bradley's manic depression pushed him to the edge.

"I hate my job," she would say. This was a common prelude to hours of venting about the state of things in the daycare, hours of venting Bradley did his best to sit through. Eventually he found himself a job selling mattresses. It wasn't the best, but he sat down with Sarah on the couch after work one day.

"Hey, babe. I hate this mattress job but I can make it work. Find yourself something else to do, maybe wait tables or something. I can handle the bills for a while, then find my dream job once you've found something better."

But Sarah refused. She kissed Bradley and went to bed.

A few weeks came and went, and she grew sullen as she drank more and more. Still possessing an extreme hatred for her present employment, she now lacked an audience because Bradley had to work sixty hours per week. He wasn't home until 9:00 most nights. She had to be at work at 7:00 in the morning, so the couple only spent an hour or so together in the evening before it was time for her to go to bed. Bradley came home to find her drunk more often than not. On Tuesdays and Thursdays, he went to classes at a local community college. When Sarah got home, he'd try to get her to do something that didn't involve wine, but she only went along with it because he wasn't there to stop her any other night.

Still, he tried to lighten things a bit. His boss, Ebony, was a large woman who was even meaner than she looked. He nicknamed her Ebenezer for Sarah's amusement, and was stunned when she fired him a week before Christmas. Sarah clinched her teeth and told him it was a good thing she hadn't quit her job.

Her face darkened. Fierce arguments had only recently become part of their relationship, but she wanted to avoid another one. "I don't want to be part of a relationship like my parents', where we just fight all the time," she said.

Bradley knew it had to end long before it did, and perhaps Sarah did as well. Sarah's depression had swelled as her healing mother stormed back into her life. Theirs had been a caustic relationship before college, before the tumor. It was less so, now, and Sarah badly wanted her mother to come back, sweeter and more friendly after her operation. Unfortunately, Elizabeth had changed little. Bradley's frustration at what he saw as Sarah's refusal to stay true to herself swelled until, one night early in January, she asked him to go for a run.

He agreed, and headed home from his job search. Sitting on the couch in running shorts, he smiled as

Sarah walked into the small apartment. She sat down, picked up her laptop, and surfed the internet until it was almost dark. He elected to go for his run alone.

Getting madder with every step along the path, he was too angry to speak when he returned to the apartment. He finally had the opportunity to actually find work, now the holidays were over, and she was both an antagonist and a stumbling block. To make matters worse, he had found a dating app on her computer. She denied it was something she'd installed intentionally, but he wasn't stupid. Finally, the door to the apartment was in front of him. He pushed it open. She sat on the couch, holding her laptop.

"We need to talk. Let's go get something to eat."

The couple got in the car and drove to a small, sit down Chinese place down the street. Bradley had his thoughts in order, but Sarah spoke first.

"I can't believe you haven't found a job yet. Put your pride aside and work at the Subway. Work at the McDonalds. I don't care – I just need you to have a job right now."

"Look. We need to do something different. I can't have you attacking me for being unemployed and keeping me from getting a job. I don't know what you're trying to do, but tonight is a perfect example. You're just not supportive. It's like you think I can be in more than one place at a time – I can't be out looking for work and be home to entertain you at the same time."

"I try to support you, Bradley, but you won't support yourself. You don't even take the job that's right in front of you."

"I told you about that. Plus, when we went to see your parents for New Year's, we agreed to work on our relationship. That meant less time on the computer, more time hanging out and having fun. Tonight, you blew me off, after you pulled me out of the job hunt. What are you trying to do to me?"

The food came, and was eaten in relative silence.

"I was tired. I had a long day at a job I hate to pay for this fucking meal and I'm sick of it."

"Then maybe you should go home. It seems pretty obvious our relationship isn't working, and even more obvious that it's because of financial concerns. I'll be on my feet inside of a month, but you can't wait. You don't believe in me anymore. Go, then, if that's what you want to do."

They rode home in silence, and when they got back to the apartment, Sarah excused herself to make a phone call. Then she went back inside and told Bradley they were breaking off the engagement.

Bradley stands in front of the kitchen sink, paintbrush in hand. A naked canvas stares back at him. He has been talking to a barfly girl, more for his own amusement than for anything physical or emotional. Strangely enough, she is a painter. He wonders at the coincidence as he enjoys her company. She isn't what he wants, though. He only wants Sarah. He wants the Sarah he had before the tumor.

Sarah deals with her grief by dating other people, finding a steady job, and stabilizing herself. Her parents help her with each of these steps, but Bradley

141

tries to deal with it alone. For him, things do not go as smoothly. Time itself seems to flow and eddy; it seems that the current has become choppy. He wonders whether it was ever a straight line, or whether the effects of events in the future can ripple backward as well as forward along the surface of the water. Still is a funny word, he muses. Stillborn comes from a child being born which possesses no animation; a dead baby. The relationship between himself and his only great love thus far is the same – no longer moving, growing, or changing. There was no future there. It, like the child born without life, is still. Had he felt this coming? If he had, and he hadn't been able to stop it, what else was there but to be sad?

There is a dream that recurs. In it, Bradley is swimming alone at night in a lake when a thunderstorm blows in. Across the lake, as he climbs out, a tornado is bearing down on his location. He is stunned, paralyzed as it howls across the water in the lighting-punctuated blackness of a midnight Texan thunderstorm. Finally, he turns to run away – and the cone of swirling wind picks him up and throws him high into the air, over the lake. As he breaks free of the winds and begins his disoriented descent, to water, to land, to death, the dream ends and he awakens – sweating and lonely. In some distant corner of his mind, the car still idles in the parking lot and the future remains uncertain.

FOR A GOOD NIGHT'S SLEEP:

Shit, not this again. Benny mumbled to himself pretty often. He hadn't had one of these in weeks, but then again, he'd had to lay off the coffee pots and switch to just one cup a day for the past little while. He groaned and rolled over again, sleepless in the dingy old bed. He'd had a whole pot earlier, first day back at work in his store with the coffeemaker and nothing to do. Funny, it hadn't even felt hyper or fast or anything at the time – he'd sluggishly dragged himself through the day, as usual. Somehow, though, it was 4:12 in the morning and he hadn't slept a wink.

Benny got up and poured himself a drink. Then he sat there for a half hour or so, watching the idiot box try to convince him to buy a stretchy rope that would supposedly turn him into Fabio in just a week. This usually worked. Finally, he hit the power button on the remote and walked back into the kitchen for another drink. He spat on the floor, then threw a rag on top of the spit and scrubbed it up with his foot. Then he took the rag and put it into the washing machine, taking care to loudly slam the lid shut even though there wasn't a full load in yet.

Somewhere off in the distance a siren began to wail. Goddamned firemen, thought Benny, setting down the drink. There wasn't much reason for a siren like that in the middle of the goddamned night – all the streets were deserted. Didn't the fucking firemen know people were trying to sleep?

He pulled on his sweatpants, then grabbed his keys. When he got to his car, he heard the door unlock itself just before he pulled it open. He put on his seatbelt, then turned the start knob and sped off in the direction of the fire truck.

A fire truck with full lights and sirens blaring down the residential street at five in the morning is an easy thing to find. Benny was watching it from a side-street, from the far side of a park. He was racing along to come to the next intersection and give chase. He pushed the accelerator to the floor and enjoyed the burst of torque - it wouldn't be much trouble to overtake the ten-ton behemoth after that.

He looked back to the road ahead, applying the brakes and running a stop sign to quickly skid around a corner. He wasn't completely through the turn when he put the accelerator back on the floor, and the car fishtailed a bit. Benny was grinning from ear to ear, enjoying the chase. Suddenly, he ran over a jogger.

Goddamnit, Benny thought, parking the car. Maybe instead of ran over, ran under might be a better term. The poor bastard had been running in the fucking road with it dark outside, at least up until Benny clipped his legs from under him at fifty or sixty miles per hour. Then he'd been flung up onto the hood of the car, rolled over the windshield and roof, and dropped to a crumpled heap on the pavement.

Benny checked the guy for a pulse. Nothing. Benny checked the guy's pockets, but all he found was a damned mp3 player. No cell phone. Benny checked to see if he'd brought his. Nothing in his own pockets, maybe it was in the car. He idly knocked the guy's tennis shoe from the hood of his car down to the street, gazing back at the crumpled heap on the pavement. Where was his cell phone when he actually needed it?

He got back into the car and started the engine, still hunting for the goddamned phone. Just like the fucking thing to have gotten itself misplaced during the only emergency in which he'd ever really needed it.

Oh well, Benny thought. Guy's dead, anyway.

When he got home, the light in his covered parking space revealed that there was no real damage to his car – no blood, no dents, no guts. He scratched his head and went inside to go and find the phone. It wasn't on the kitchen table. Or on the couch. He went into the bedroom to check the nightstand where he usually left it to charge while he slept. Yep. There it was. Right next to the big, comfortable bed. Suddenly exhausted, Benny collapsed on the bed and slept well into the next day.

DREAMING OF YOU

I sat on the porch, smoking cigarettes. It was a warm August day and my arthritis was acting up again. Willie, my next-door neighbor, carried a black garbage bag out of his house and deposited it in the trash barrel out by the curb. He dusted his hands off, rubbing them together, and walked over to my porch.

"Hello, Thelma."

He took a seat opposite me at the table. We sat in silence for a moment.

"Hi Willie. Lemonade?" I poured myself another glass from the pitcher that sat on the table between us. Willie considered, but it seemed to require a bit of thought. He waited a moment to answer.

"No, thanks. Pretty day, isn't it?"

"Yessir. Beautiful." I took a long sip from my glass, and we sat in silence for a few moments.

"How's your arthritis?" Something else was on his mind, but I wasn't sure what it might be. He stood up, preparing to leave even though we had only passed a few minutes together.

"Oh, you know. Same old thing day after day. It's a wonder ole arthritis hasn't given up and gone on to torment some other soul."

Willie chuckled a bit.

"Let me know if there's anything I can do to help."

He stepped off the porch.

"You take care, William."

"You too, Thelma. Hope things get to feelin' better."

I had no idea where he was headed in such a hurry. I had planned to tell him about my nightmares. After all, he was the star. Dreams rarely come true in this world and I hope, for Willie's sake, that a silly old nightmare is all it was.

I knew Willie was a young man who lived recklessly and enjoyed every minute of the chaos he brought upon himself. He wasn't afraid of anything at all and he smoked, drank and did everything else too. He had a lot of ambition but very little direction and it was a hard time on him, since his father passed under strange circumstances in the shed behind their house. I knew Willie had inherited a small fortune, but wasn't particularly interested in money. He just lived there, in the nice suburban home on the outskirts of Georgetown. He drove down to Austin to see friends and raise hell, and we looked after each other. I helped him with his hangovers and he came by to check on me. He was always very nice to me, a good-hearted young man.

I met Willie when his father passed away. I had just moved to town because my son, Randy, wanted to care for me after dear old Larry's passing. He lived in Austin, but the house was too small and too busy for my taste. They left me all alone in a nice, big house with a maid that came twice a week. When the cops and ambulances and firetrucks all drove away from the house that now belonged to Willie, I had walked over there with a pie. Willie had needed a great deal of consolation and we quickly became friends – until I tried to tell him about the dreams I'd been having. He must have thought I was crazy. He was still a friend and came by to sit on the porch with me every day, but it was a difficult relationship to maintain because we had next to nothing in common. I was still glad he bothered himself to come by and see me though, very sweet young man that he was.

The questions his mind came up with were probably my favorite part of the young man. I didn't approve of his partying but that was his concern; my part was to support him as much as I could and help him get through this rough patch.

One day, he had asked me if I believed in God. Of course I did, and told him so, and asked whether or not he did. He told me that God was certainly real, but I knew for a fact he hadn't set foot in a church in years. I'd asked him about it, and he told me he'd grown up Catholic. Studying the scriptures in-depth. He'd concluded that they were meant to be taken metaphorically, and that God wasn't some separate being – that God was what you got when you added all the people and animals and world up together. All the consciousness, maybe.

I asked if he believed in the afterlife, and he responded with a riddle.

"Well, Thelma," I remembered this moment as if it were just yesterday. "I've got a question for you too: do you think people in heaven have bodies?"

I'd been a little confused, but I knew enough scripture to know that it sure wasn't similar to the way things were down here. I said something along those lines, and he laughed.

"Good for you. People are really just their bodies, and their conscious minds. A conscious mind is a strange thing, though, and when you think about it, our various interactions with the world around us are really all we know about. I can't decide I don't like Rush Limbaugh if I never hear the name of the man, if I never see him, if I never get sucked into a conversation about him." He paused, wondering if I was following him.

"Yes, that's true. Don't you think there's something inside of us, though? A soul?" I was on the edge of my seat, waiting for the response.

"Well, I do, but only as mediated by my interactions with culture and with other people and with books and things like that. But let me tell you something else: these interactions change people. They change their bodies, their brains, the thoughts they think, everything. When my body dies, I suppose I won't have new experiences anymore – but that doesn't mean that other people will quit experiencing the effects of my life."

"But what about you, Willie? Where do you go?" I asked. I felt as though I was missing part of his point.

"That's the thing, Thelma. I only get a certain amount of time to experience things, but my reactions to them change the world around me forever. You know what they say, that if a butterfly flaps its wings in Cuba it can cause a hurricane to hit New York. Life is sacred, and valuable. Our impacts upon others are the only way our existence is ever known to begin with - these events are formative, and have far greater consequences than any of us can fathom. Life is fragile, yet resilient."

"So every point in my life is the most important point there could be? What if someone doesn't like something I do? If that is what God disapproving of me is, I won't have a very happy life!"

"There is a difference between being unmoved by trivial events and discounting the unfathomable depths of meaning each of us possesses and creates simply by being." Willie sat back, and didn't say anything else. He lit a cigarette and took a drink of his lemonade. I'd thanked him for his conversation, and told him I needed to think about it more.

I had no idea I'd even fallen asleep. It was a good nap, too. The pain seemed mostly gone when I awakened in my comfortable rocking chair. God was on my mind when I got up and went into the house. Such a nice house, picture of Larry above the fireplace, beautiful hardwood floors. There were a few rooms I hadn't even been inside yet but I didn't take the time to explore them now. Instead I walked my tired self into the kitchen and set some water to boil on the stove for tea.

I looked through the pantry, and in the refrigerator. There was tea, and I made myself a cup, but as I drank it I wrote out a shopping list. The kitchen was nearly empty. I looked for the car keys and found them on a hook next to the door. It was time for a grocery run. I backed the car out of the garage and down the driveway, but then Willie ran up and banged on the window.

"William, how are you?" I asked, opening the window.

"I'm doing well. Are you going somewhere?" he asked in return.

"Well, I need groceries. Would you like to come along? You're a better driver than I am."

"Alright," he said, walking around to the driver's side of the car.

As we drove, the silence built up until I couldn't hold my tongue anymore.

"Willie, about these dreams I've been havin'. I'm an old lady and you listen to me young man. I'm not telling you to do anything just listen – you need to know."

"Alright Thelma. I hope it's happier than the last one."

"William, these aren't good dreams. I don't know if it means anything to you but I dreamt Larry's death before it happened and there have been others. There are spirits in this world that nobody wants to know about. They aren't really here like all the scientists and doctors look for. I've seen those shows on the TV and they can't find what they're lookin' for because they look for the wrong things. Only thing tells you if there's something around that's not supposed to be is your own body. Now, in my dreams you're always wearing a white suit and you're in a church, I think. Then you say a few words and I wake up screamin', feelin' emotions that don't quite fit – I'm terrified, Willie. I wake up terrified and there never is a reason why."

"Next the legs go." He burst out laughing, and so did I. He helped me shop, and the tone remained light. I was glad to have him there with me.

The next week the dream was back, except longer and with a few new details. I was waking up because the dream's focus shifted away from Willie, to me, and I was falling. I was horrified. I decided to avoid Willie as much as possible. I started smoking cigarettes inside and I didn't go out for any reason. Willie came by each day to check on me, but I was too afraid to answer the door.

That Sunday I went to church to see if the Lord would offer me guidance. I had no proof that Willie was capable of killing me or giving me bad dreams and maybe it was just some devil tryin' to steel me against my only friend. If there was a message for me to find in the sermon, I didn't get it. It was an argument about why it was okay for folks to raise their hands during worship, whatever that was. Damned Southern Christians. I hated them for getting between me and my God when I needed him the most. I didn't talk to anybody and I left just as soon as I heard that sermon because it told me forget all this Jesus hocus-pocus that the numbskulls were getting into these days.

I went straight over to Willie's house after church. He was sleeping off what must have been one hell of a hangover, considering it was after noon. I knocked loud, and he didn't answer. So, I knocked again and one more time, still no answer. I tried the doorknob

153

and went inside when it was unlocked. I found Willie layin' on his side next to the car in the garage, a big puddle of vomit next to his unconscious body. I slapped him a few times 'til he woke up and told him to come inside and lay down in the bed like a good boy. Then I cleaned up and went home again to pass a few hours while the poor boy slept. When I got back over there a bit before sundown I had a few questions for Willie.

"Thanks for waking me this morning," he yawned. "And for cleaning up the mess and bringing me water. I was worried about you not being around for a while, did your family pick you up or something?" Willie looked green, but at least he was sitting up and speaking.

"Yeah, that's it child. I was glad to see 'em and I'll tell you next time I leave town if you want me to. Thank you for caring about me. I wanted to ask you about the dream again. I know it's not your favorite thing to talk about, but it's getting worse."

"Okay. I'm really just weirded out by the way you talk about me acting in that dream you always have – are you sure it's even me in it?" I made a face. He shrugged a bit. "Oh sorry, didn't mean to sidebar. What's new in the dream?"

Willie didn't mean no disrespect. He was a good boy. Of course, I was sure it was him in the dream.

"I wanted to tell you that I woke up from one with a better memory of the thing – I ended it by falling. The dream took this sudden turn from you doin' your talking to me takin' a nasty fall. I'm the next one who's going to die, Willie. I think you should wear a white suit to my funeral and give my family a nice eulogy to remember me by. You're the first true friend I have had in a long time, you know. I think it would be nice for them to know how good we've had it, looking after each other these past months."

"Okay, Thelma. Sounds good to me – but you aren't going anywhere anytime soo-" His sentence cut off when he realized I wasn't listening anymore.

I smiled because I had figured out what the dream meant! It was a real happy feelin'. Suddenly my vision blurred and I heard Willie screamin' "Thelma! What's going on? Are you okay?" and so forth. I don't know what he meant yelling those things – but I realized I was laying on the floor now. The world was fadin' away from me. I couldn't hear much, but I saw Willie leanin' over me. Poor sweet boy. He looked worried. When I shut my eyes, I knew they'd never open again.

BLACK DRESS

"Hi, there. What's your name?" She had radiant brown eyes and short blonde hair. Her pouty lips pursed themselves when she finished speaking. Her little black dress beautifully accented her tanned skin and clung to the sublime curves of her body.

"Trent," I replied. I was dressed up, wearing a button up shirt and a pair of black slacks with my sneakers. I took a drag from my cigarette. "And yours?" I let the smoke cascade out from my nose for dramatic effect.

The full, healthy lips parted to make way for a smile. A manicured hand with black nail polish reached for mine.

"Tiffany," she said.

I nodded, my eyes glued to hers.

"So," she continued, "Trent, are you having a good time?"

"Never better," I said. "I just got published."

"Oh, that's great! Where?"

I took another drag from my cigarette.

"The Superfluity Literary Talent Review. They bought a poem of mine."

"What was it about?"

I looked away, trying to decide whether or not to tell her the truth.

"Not getting published."

I took a sip of my drink, then met her eyes again.

"Making lemonade, eh?"

I couldn't help it. I smiled.

"Oh, yeah. It's almost superfluous at this point. I have a job and I'm looking into grad school."

Her eyebrows raised themselves.

"Really? What for?"

"Well, I work so I can pay bills. I want to go back to school because I find the students interesting."

She chuckled a bit.

"No, I meant what will you study."

"Oh, okay." I winked at her. "Philosophy, probably. That's all I ever seem to end up studying."

"Oh, ok. What's your favorite philosophy?"

"Ha. Well, philosophy is a tool you use to look at ideas. Like a more practical kind of math. I suppose humanity seems to be moving toward a hedonistic, egoistic anarchy. It makes me happy, we should have done it years ago."

"Well, that's nice. I like smart guys."

She moved in close.

"Do you want to dance?"

Her perfume smelled of heaven.

"No, thank you."

She turned back, as she walked away, smiling to me. That was when I realized I'd lost my mind.

THE POINT

There is a man who sits on a mountain in the country of Laicep who knows why the world is about to end. He understands why things seem to be accelerating at a thunderous pace, always moving faster than the day, year or decade previous. The veiled push for primitivism on a large scale has always been motivated by a kind of desperation, a manic urgency that denies the importance of *this* life, *this* people. The feeling reduces men to psychopaths bent upon the murder of brothers, he reflects. He sits, eyes closed, meditating upon the end of the world as snow falls around him.

His eyes are open in a different place, away from his physical body. In this place, he *is* the mountain. In this place, his soul is as immutable and unmovable as a continent, as large and daunting as a metropolis. There are stars in the sky, and there is earth underfoot – a vast, dead plain of matter that is as invisible as the floor of a deep ocean or the very core of the earth in our physical world.

It is a world that has been built up, over the generations and mutations and evolutions of life forms; beginning, as always, with the simplest. Even as single celled organisms relate to the complexities of mammalian creatures in the physical world, their souls relate to the souls of men in the spiritual one where the man now looks around. Everything shines with a different color of light; and light comes only from life. Even as souls flicker out and collapse, they are covered over by seas of the living.

The man studied physics, once. A main sequence star has a definite life cycle. It burns hydrogen first, fusing it into heavier elements. Eventually, the elements have been fused to a point of no return – there aren't enough light ones left for fuel – and the star dies; first expanding, then contracting so as to spew matter out to form other things.

That doesn't seem to be how it is here, in this world of dark mass and brilliant light. The stars in the sky represent other places where this phenomenon takes place in the spiritual world, he thinks as he patiently observes the world around him. There is no real motion in a physical sense, no body to move. Only possibility, composed of monads large and small, monads that grow without eating, never consume one another, and winkle into existence from nothingness. As he looks around with human eyes, he sees a certain formlessness to the world surrounding him. Lumpy, yet expansive. It is fortunate he sits in a high place, for he is unable to move about.

Oddly enough, he thinks, the man begins to recognize people he knows in the soup of lights nearest him. A man he studied with sits twinkling amongst a thousand larger and smaller souls, but is certainly recognizable. A wave, a thought, a feeling of recognition passes through him and he tries to stand.

Back on top of the mountain, his physical eyes open. He stands, freezing, covered in freshly fallen snow, and walks a short way to a building where his brothers live. Inside, he finds soup, a fire, and friendly faces; but he does not smile. He does not sit by the fire to chase away his chill, and he does not drink warm soup to fill his stomach. He sits away from his fellows, facing a wall, saying nothing.

In the spiritual world, there is no sound as the mountain collapses upon itself. There is no moment of darkness; for even as his soul winks out others have already appeared to cover it over. Soon, the mountain he represented is taller than before, covered thick with the brightly shining lights of the living.

His brothers approach him, and finding him dead, begin to prepare his body for the funeral pyre.

Far, far away an old spirit-star grows dark, but it does not explode. It simply... continues, without its light. And elsewhere, in the night, a new light begins to shine. Slowly, at first, each light the same color as each other as they wink into existence. Soon, as they all get farther away, there are other colors and the source grows brighter, stronger.

From the proper vantage point, anyone who spoke English could read the vivid, flashing, cosmic scale neon sign. Every life form in the universe served the purpose of illuminating this sign, a scrolling banner that looked as if it were composed of LEDs that repeated the same message, over and over.

This is what it said:

So, THIS is the point of everything?

A few days later, the other monks were going through their deceased brother's possessions and

161

deciding what to do with the few meager robes and scraps of clothing when they found a single page covered with the following text, written in their brother's small, precise hand:

What, exactly, do we mean when we say conscious, or alive? Alive is a strange word that cannot truly be approached by science because science deals with building blocks and alive is something more; animated might be a way to describe it. Looking at the universe from the perspective of a beam of light, two things should be perfectly obvious: no distance and no time. Light seems to hold the key for philosophers to an even greater extent than for the physicists.

When the amount of energy something has can be equated to the amount of mass it has times the speed of light, the overwhelming contradiction that is evident lies within the very fabric of the veil over humanity's eyes.

Conclusions first, the way an honest man argues: the universe cannot be dated. Light travels to earth instantly because, according to the Lorentz contraction, an observer viewing an object traveling at the speed of light would be viewing an object that had, literally, no length in the current frame of reference. To say light travels is very close to fallacy, however, when the full implications of this revelation come to light: given that a particle traveling the speed of light has no length, it is also true that the distance it travels has no length. From the standpoint of a beam of light, everything is essentially at the same place, at the same time.

To further muddy the waters of relativistic physics, the commonly dated universe must also be fallacy. Though simultaneity is debunked by Einstein, we can consider time measuring to be 'current and ongoing.'

Perhaps the most damning argument science has put forth against the use of common sense to attack problems is the simple statement that everything we see, everything we are, is in the present.

It is not an argument to be made by a physicist, but the evidence is nonetheless apparent.

P1. Alive is a state that describes growth – a one-way street.

P2. We are unable to rationally analyze life itself because it never exists except with respect to certain objects; it is accepted to be impossible that, once truly dead, a body should come back to life and it is simply preposterous to argue that life can exist without a body.

P3. The Theory of Relativity and the Lorentz contraction combine to prove that, though light has a speed, its distance to travel amounts to nothing.

P4. The Theory of Relativity also proves time passage relative to frame of reference.

P5. An age factor cannot be assigned to the universe as a whole because it consists of many different frames of reference, all of which have different time and therefore have existed longer or shorter relative to one another – but of course if motion is to be taken into account, this must potentially be a two-way street – which not only argues in favor of the 'infinite universe' theory but also lends a hand in proving that our conception of time is fundamentally flawed.

C1: Human consciousness exists only in the present, as alive. For example, me writing this. The state of mind that caused me to write that will never repeat itself because change of other variables has taken place since the incident took place. Essentially, the present can be seen to stand still as the world moves around it; and any attempt a self-aware consciousness makes to explain the world is based upon a present impression of an object being sensed or a memory from the past which is in no necessary way bound to the present moment - aside from the present stream of consciousness. Essentially, these streams of consciousness skipping from moment to moment are what we can understand as alive.

Alive, then, is an ordering of events that are characterized by growth as well as being relative to a singular perspective and a sequence of presents. The arc of a thrown ball before it strikes the earth, the surge of a lightning strike, the apparent motion of a wave on the ocean. Ironically, alive can reflect upon itself, *but it cannot give away its secrets – for the truth is that order is imposed by alive upon everything else, but not because alive things are stronger or better than the other things. Things that have life, that are alive, that are aware of themselves - they order the world because their mere existence adds a frame of reference to the world; through which the information available there and then must be interpreted by that entity - because beings that live simply possess no other way of interacting with their surroundings. Even plants can fit this alive definition, whereas inanimate objects fail because the plant is a system of self-order.*

C2: Our world is orders of magnitude more complex than our present understanding of it.

If the information their brother had written down puzzled them, they did not show it. Instead, they locked the manuscript away.

A Note From the Author:

You can find more information about new releases, upcoming events, and other developments at my press site, thomasdylandaniel.press, or on Facebook at facebook.com/tdylandaniel.

I have written one other book at this point. It is called *Formal Dialectics* and is a more serious philosophy book. Still, it has been written for the layperson, and I would encourage anyone who enjoyed *Further From Home* to have a look at it.

Again, I appreciate your interest in my work. This book is what I like to think of as "street philosophy" – a hodgepodge of Zen and more serious philosophical concepts. I hope you enjoyed reading it as much as I enjoyed writing it. It was mainly composed in chunks over the course of my twenties, and I like to think that's when a lot of learning went on for me.

Thank you for your support!

Cheers,

T.   Dylan   Daniel

ABOUT THE AUTHOR:

Thomas Dylan Daniel is a free-thinking Texan philosopher with degrees from Southwestern University and Texas State University. *Further From Home* is his first book of short fiction. His essays appear in *Oil, Gas & Energy Law* as well as *PhilosophyNow* and *Philosophy of Language* (ed. Brian Thomas, 2015). His second book, *Formal Dialectics*, is available now from Cambridge Scholars Publishing.

Key research interests include philosophy of language, philosophy of mind, and ethics, as well as cognitive neuroscience, artificial intelligence, machine learning, and environmental science.

Printed in Great Britain
by Amazon